THE PLAYERS' BOY IS DEAD

A Matthew Stock Mystery

By Leonard Tourney

"This detective story, written in the style of 16th-century England, is vividly evocative of its era."

People

"This exceptional mystery comes from . . . an English professor who plotted murder while doing background reading for a Shakespeare course."

Jean M. White
The Washington Post

"Tourney is a superb writer, skilled in the richness of the Elizabethan use of the language."

The Tulsa World

Also by Leonard Tourney
Published by Ballantine Books:

THE BARTHOLOMEW FAIR MURDERS

THE PLAYERS' BOY IS DEAD

Leonard Tourney

BALLANTINE BOOKS · NEW YORK

Originally published, in hardcover, by Harper & Row, Publishers, Inc. in 1980.

Library of Congress Catalog Card Number: 80-7611

ISBN 0-345- 34371-9

Manufactured in the United States of America

First Ballantine Books Edition: June 1988

1

BEFORE the first crow of the cock the scullery maid at the Triple Crown awoke to the rustle of mice in the thatch and the moon flowing through the cracks in the timbers like strands of golden wire. She lay motionless, savoring the warmth of the straw and the solace of a half-remembered dream; then she rose stolidly. There were no windows in the shed, and the tiny room was close and retained the fetid odor of its previous occupants: a brace of fine geese, since sold to the butcher. It would have been as black as the devil's heart had it not been for the moon. She pulled her shawl around her shoulders, brushed the loose straw from her hair, and crossed herself twice before going out into the empty yard.

The moon was indeed full, sailing in its pride, filling the yard with somber yellow light. The inn itself was still dark, for as usual she had been the first one to rise. She walked over to the well, drew water, and doused her face and neck. She would have liked to return to her warm place in the straw, to the intense, almost physical pleasure of her dream. But there would be none of that. Master Rowley had beaten her twice for lingering abed.

It was time to wake Simon the hostler, to slop the pigs,

and to join Tabitha and May in the kitchen before the inn-keeper awoke. She thought of the long day ahead and sighed heavily, forgetting the desolation of the moon-filled yard, the chill of late October, and her dream.

She had been a child when she had first come to the inn two years before, sparrow-timid and tearful. Tom, the innkeeper's son had teased her mercilessly, ridiculing her slow, languid movements and her halting speech, and playing all manner of tricks on her. He had once put a dead rat in her cap so that when she had reached for it her fingers grasped the creature's tail and she had screamed, bringing Tabitha the cook on the run with a meat cleaver in her hand and a fearsome oath on her lips that had stopped Tom cold. "Leave the girl be," Tabitha had stormed.

"I done her no harm," the large raw-boned youth had sputtered, visibly shaken by this sudden burst of female violence.

After that Tom had left her alone, and sometime later he had died of the fever.

The girl had grown taller now, looked less the boy. She would be fourteen soon, and already her breasts were fuller than her mother's. She was proud of her black hair, how it glistened long and thick upon her shoulders, and of the blush of her fair, clear skin. She took delight in the wistful stares of the inn's gentleman patrons, and even in the mute envy of Tabitha and May, plain girls with raw red hands, mottled complexions, and close-set quizzical eyes.

When the cock crowed at last, she hurried across the yard to the stable. Simon the hostler was old, blind in one eye, and lame. He had been a soldier by his own account, had fought at Zutphen, where poor Sir Philip Sidney died. But that had been fifteen years before. Now his breath always reeked of garlic and his voice creaked like two branches rubbing each other in a storm. She pulled open the door and ventured in. The stable was pitch black, but she could smell animals and men and hear someone snoring and tossing fitfully in the first stall. She called Simon's name softly—she did not want to wake the players, who also made their beds in the stable. The night before she had heard their laughter as they had returned from the great house. *They* would not soon be rising, full as they were of Sir Henry's cheer and master Marlowe's poetry.

The horses were already awake and moving restlessly as she felt her way to the first stall. Beneath her feet a human body stirred. She whispered Simon's name again. A shapeless thing in the straw mumbled and coughed. It rose before her, stooped, and cursed her beneath its breath.

"Damn the master who orders me to wake you," she said, holding her voice steady, not wanting to show fear. "The master's saddle must be mended by noon and Lady shoed, and the gentleman merchant from London and his wife will be abroad before breakfast and their horses must be readied."

"The master's saddle must be mended," Simon said, mimicking her. "Why, I wonder that the master should want aught at all, being so fortunate as he is to have thee, girl." The hostler lurched toward her, reached out, and pinched her cheek.

She drew back in alarm and disgust. "He'll beat you soundly if he finds out you've touched me," she said, her voice quivering.

Simon chuckled to himself. "Do you believe in the devil?" he said.

But the hostler did not wait for an answer, nor did the girl give one. He fumbled around for his coat and cap, snatched them up violently from where they lay in the straw, and thrust her aside.

She stood for a moment in the darkness watching the hostler stumble across the moonlit yard, then touched her cheek tenderly and fought to hold back tears of anger and pain. She hated Simon, even more than she hated the master. She had felt no pity when the players had called the old man into the firelight and Samuel Peacham had poured the hot candle wax down his shirt. It was a rough jest, and Simon had screamed like a wounded animal, like a stuck pig. The players had roared with laughter, Will Shipman's great chest heaving beneath his

3

russet jerkin and his black beard still wet with the wine, while Richard had sat pensively in the corner, his face strangely sad.

Her cheek hurt less now and she peered curiously into the darkness of the stable. Somewhere beyond, the players were sleeping. How queer players were, she reflected as she moved down the line of dark stalls—like the fairies in which she half believed and sometimes spied peeking from behind the ferns at the pool's edge. The players had brought into her life music and laughter and a vision of things as they might be. And more, for Will Shipman had said that being a player was as good as being a scholar, for while a scholar might know Latin, yet a player must know the heart. Richard knew the heart; he knew hers, she was sure. And a player who knew hearts might end well with proper land, a fair house, and a comely wife. Will Shipman had said all of that, and winked at her and at Richard too. She had laughed at his words, as though to dismiss them as a bauble, but inside she had felt inexpressible joy.

The stable was long and low-ceilinged, and most of the stalls were empty or full of trash. She heard the sound of the men before she could see them, their bodies scattered in the straw of the rear stalls like piles of rags. There was no mistaking Will Shipman. The chief player lay on his back, his chest rising and falling rhythmically, his full beard indistinguishable in the half light from the thick mat of hair on his chest. His muscular arms were stretched out to each side, and his head was cocked toward one shoulder like the picture of Our Lord she had once seen in the priest's book.

She stepped over the bodies carefully, looking for Richard now. She did not wish to wake him; she only wanted a glimpse of him asleep. It was a girl's longing she had, something that made her suddenly forget Simon's viciousness and the dreariness of the day before her.

Richard Mull was the players' boy. He was fourteen and he acted the women's parts because he was slender and fair and his voice had the soft treble of a woman's. In the week the company had been in the town, Richard had shown the girl some small courtesies. He had spoken gently to her, kissed and fondled her by the firelight, allowed her, when Will Shipman wasn't looking, to dress herself in the rich velvet gowns Richard wore on the stage. He had given her reason to hope, and she had given her heart to him even though he had not asked for it. Fearful of ridicule, she had confided her love to no one, although perhaps Will Shipman sensed it.

Her father had long ago run off to sea and had probably drowned by now; her mother, had she known the way her daughter's heart was leaning, would have beaten her soundly. But she would have beaten her in vain. The Triple Crown was a luckless place, half empty even in travelers' season, and yet it had broadened the girl's horizon. Now the names of the great towns—and especially London—rang in her head like church bells on Sunday. There, to London, Richard Mull would take her, and Simon the hostler might sleep until the Judgment and the innkeeper's rushes go unchanged until Easter. But until she should be delivered from this place, the girl resolved to keep Richard hidden in the secret places of her heart. Even the old priest would not know, he who nodded quietly and wisely at her confession as though half asleep and spoke her penance without rancor.

Now in the gathering light she moved more confidently. Big Tod and Little Tod lay side by side. She could see the pockmarks on Little Tod's face, how his brows turned upward at the ends and how his nostrils bristled with hairs. His sharp pointed nose twitched nervously and his whole body gave little jerks, like a hanged man dancing on a rope. And there was Samuel Peacham curled up against the wall, his knees brought up protectively against his chest.

But she did not see Richard.

She counted the bodies again. Will Shipman, the brothers Tod, and Samuel Peacham—four, leaving only Richard Mull missing.

The men were beginning to stir, and she was about to turn when her eye caught something white and glistening in the last stall. As she approached it, she saw that it was the players' boy. He was sitting with his back to a bale of hay, his arms and chest bare; and as she drew closer still, she could see that his eyes were open, rolled upward, as though he were watching something in the beams of the ceiling or caught up in some ecstasy.

2

A<small>N HOUR</small> after the scullery maid at the inn had found the players' boy dead, Matthew Stock unbolted the door of his new shop on High Street for the day's business. From the several floors above occupied by Master Stock, his wife, and various household servants and apprentices he could hear Dame Joan directing Alice and Betty to the airing of the beds, while in the back parts of the shop the weavers were already at their looms and the place humming with industry. Outside, young Tom the apprentice, having swept the threshold, was preparing to wash down the cobblestone pavement.

Like its owner, the shop had a distinct look of prosperity. Trestle tables groaned under the load of bolt upon bolt of newly woven cloth with which their owner did a brisk business both in town and country, indeed carrying his goods as far as London. The little clothier himself dressed plainly, in an old-fashioned way. A dark, thickset man in his early forties, Matthew was blessed with an industrious wife who ordered her household with the same managerial competence as did her husband his shop. Like her husband, she was dark and plump, though her face had a fine oval shape. She wore her hair in a bun, after the Spanish fashion. They had a daughter named Elizabeth, who had recently married well and who, the couple expected, would any day announce herself with child.

The Stocks, man and wife for twenty years, were devoted to one another. Their weekdays were given to what each considered the serious business of life, putting bread on the table for themselves and those whom God had placed in their charge and living decently and loyally as was no more than to be expected of subjects of the Queen of England and the King of Heaven. On Sundays they heard Master Whittington preach, and after service would sometimes walk to the end of High Street and into the country for several miles before returning to a shoulder of lamb and March beer. Both could read; and Matthew was a musician with a richly resonant tenor voice that gave his neighbors on the street much pleasure.

Matthew Stock had begun in a modest way, as apprentice to an older and distant cousin. From him Matthew had learned the clothier's trade, to keep accounts, and to treat his customers courteously. For twenty-five years he had kept shop in the older section of the town in a building much too small for either his goods or his ambitions; and having prospered, he had in recent months built a handsome house of four stories and a spacious attic, reserving the ground floor for his shop.

High Street was narrow and crooked, running generally east to west except where the river ran through the town and the street made an abrupt curve to accommodate a stone bridge. From there the street wound its way a half mile toward a hill, and then into the open country. Matthew's house shared the end of the street with several others of stout oak timber and plaster, facing each other stolidly across a passage of such narrowness that it was locally held that friendly neighbors might shake each other by the hand from the upper story. To the rear of Matthew's house was a small pasture and several outbuildings: a privy, barn, and warehouse. In a corner of the pasture, Joan kept a clamorous flock of geese, ducks, and hens, which, as she had explained to her husband, were better than a brace of hounds at warning of sturdy beggars or runaway apprentices on moonless nights.

Matthew ran his fingers over the smoothly woven fabric, the Coggeshall whites for which the clothiers of Essex had become known throughout England, stacked in bolts so near to the low ceiling that despite the large casement window at the front of the shop he often found it necessary to light lamps at noonday. He heard the clatter of William and Mark at the looms, and the voices of Tom and Peter Bench as they prepared goods for next market day.

The bell at the door tinkled frantically. Behind him he heard the thud of footfalls over bare planking.

The young, slender man with pale pockmarked face and colorless close-set eyes did not wait for Matthew to greet him. "You keep shop early, Master Stock."

"I am no sooner about my business than you, Master Varnell, it would seem."

The young man cleared his throat, balancing himself upon the balls of his feet as though he had just stepped ashore after a month at sea.

"May I interest you in a bolt of cloth, for a suit perhaps?" Matthew ventured.

"I am here in an official way, not for goods."

"In an official way?"

"Sir Henry has sent me to call you to your duty as constable. There has been a murder at the Triple Crown. One of the players was found dead this morning."

"At the inn, you say, one of the players?" the clothier echoed with astonishment. "Why, how did the man die?"

"Disemboweled," the secretary replied matter-of-factly, admiring his own hands, which were white and clean in the dim light of the shop. "His body was left naked in the stable, found by a maid and the chief player, a Master Shipman. The murderer and his motives are left to you to discover, if you can."

"I pray God I may," the little clothier declared with amazement, "for such a death falls heavily upon us, though he that was murdered was not of this place."

The younger man appraised the older one coolly. "Well," he said, sighing skeptically, "Sir Henry trusts

9

you competent in this business, and your townsmen have called you to your office. You may report to the Hall later in the day what you find."

"Indeed I will," Matthew said as the other man turned on his heels and abruptly departed.

The bell tinkled again. "A queer sort, he. Who was he?" his wife asked as she descended the stairs.

"His lordship's new secretary, Peter Varnell."

"In faith," she said brusquely, "he has an unseemly pinched face and womanish manner. What was his business?"

Matthew shared the news with his wife, upon which she crossed herself and exclaimed, "God help us!"

"You," she continued once she had caught her breath, "are to inquire into the murder?"

"I am," he replied.

"Well," she said, as though she had made up her own mind to ask Matthew to do it, "I'll fetch your cloak. Look you dress warm against the cold, for one death to this town this day is enough."

When she returned with his cloak and hat, she said, "And how long may this business keep you, Master Constable?"

"I know not, but since Sir Henry Saltmarsh is magistrate, his business may keep me as long as it might please him. Today therefore you must run the shop. If Martin Simpson should ask for his goods, you may give him what credit he desires. I know him to be honest."

"I trust you do not fear my management," she said with that particular sharpness of tongue Matthew recognized as more than half jest.

"I think, on the contrary, that I shall be the richer," he replied, smiling.

She laughed and embraced her husband affectionately. "Godspeed, Master Constable, and look that while you lead the hue and cry that you watch for your own safety. I should be much sorrowed if I had to replace you."

He took her face in his hands and kissed her hard upon the lips. "And I should be sorry if anything but a good old age were to take me from your side, Joan. Pray God we have many good years left together before our story be done.''

A gray sky threatened rain. He secured the fastenings of his cloak and pressed his hat firmly upon his head against the damp air. Through the crooked street he walked briskly, past the silversmith's, the grocer and bondsman, the scrivener's shop with the new sign. In a corner of the street a gaggle of tardy schoolboys clustered in a ring chanting an old song of the country. At his approach the boys fled, laughing all the while. Mistress Blount, who sold her penny wares from a rickety wooden cart, bid him good day; and her son, crippled, blind, and his face florid with eczema, blessed him as the constable dug into his pocket for a penny.

At the rise he paused to catch his breath and look behind him over the town, the rooftops of the houses, church steeple, and the indolent serpentine river. There were some three hundred households in Chelmsford, not counting outlying farms or Dutchmen newly arrived to work in the clothing trade. The town was prospering, there was no doubt of it. In such times as these, he reflected happily, a man willing to work, of thrifty habits and settled mind, might make something of himself and leave his sons more than a good name. Such was now being done by others. Arthur Stokes of Epping, a clothier like himself, was already possessed of more land than a hardy man could walk from sunrise to dusk.

At the end of town, High Street gave way to a narrow country lane lined with hedges of oak and hawthorn. Beyond, the lane merged with the London road, and not three miles more Matthew might see the seven chimneys of the Triple Crown, and, as he felt the first few drops of rain, the inn itself.

The Triple Crown was situated in a hollow and half-concealed from the road by a few straggling firs. It consisted of a stone building of two stories, a tavern below and lodgings above, and an innyard on the other side of which were a stable and some other small buildings. It was said that before King Henry's time the house had been a priory; if so, few signs of its earlier and more pious occupants remained. Three horses were hitched to the rail outside the inn. Smoke curled from the larger of the chimneys.

Inside, a bright fire burned on a cavernous hearth. The room was high-ceilinged, filled with benches and small tables, and empty except for two travelers drinking at the far end. They looked up as Matthew entered, then went back to their talk. A girl not more than twelve, he judged, brought him hot ale and cheese. He drank the ale slowly, putting the cheese in his pocket for later. When the girl informed him that her master was in the stable, he finished his ale, wrapped his cloak about him once more, and passed out into the yard, where the rain was now falling steadily.

He took off his hat and bent low to clear the threshold, calling out the innkeeper's name. Before him the long line of empty stalls ended in a blank wall that in the dim light he could see was hung with hostler's tools. There were no windows, and the acrid smell of human and animal urine made him draw back in disgust. The innkeeper emerged from the shadows of the first stall, stout and unsteady beneath the hulk of broad shoulders and thick bullish neck. Matthew knew the man; they had done some business together, not pleasantly.

"They played twice in the yard and to no more than a handful of gentlefolk, and them half drunk and not able to tell a codpiece from a cod. But they paid their way here for such lodgings as I gave 'em in the stable and ate no more beef nor bacon than such-like deserved. The boy was one of them, Richard Mull, but I dealt with Master Shipman, their chief. You'll want to talk to him. The boy's death is no concern of mine, save what his murder will do in giving the inn a bad name hereabouts."

Philip Rowley was but five years proprietor of the inn, during which time it had fallen from its former prosperity and respectability as a public house. His speech betrayed him a northern man, half Scot it was said, a difficult, unlikely man for an innkeeper. In his brusque speech and cold eyes, Matthew sensed the man's mute hostility to authority, his defensiveness, and feared the insolent power of his physical strength.

"Where is the body now?" Matthew asked.

"Gaze as you please," the big man snorted, jerking his head over his shoulder toward the darkness in the rear of the stable. "I must look to my own affairs."

The innkeeper pushed by him and crossed the yard to the main building. Not displeased by being left to his own devices, Matthew Stock proceeded at once to the rear stall to find on the hay-strewn floor a linen sheet the contours of which revealed the shallow outline of a human form. He bent over and pulled the covering back.

Richard Mull's eyes were shut, the muscles of the face relaxed, and Matthew saw for the first time that the dead player was indeed but a lad, with a fair face and flaxen hair that hung to the white sinewy shoulders. Matthew's eyes fell to the gaping hole where the stomach had been. The blood had dried, both upon the white skin and upon the straw. He crossed himself, replaced the covering, and hurried toward open air. He bumped against someone at the entrance.

"I have come for the boy," a man said, a big man, not with the intimidating bigness of the innkeeper but narrower in the shoulders and thicker in the middle, with ruddy face and full beard. "I am Will Shipman." Matthew stood back while the chief player bent under the door and without removing the sheet lifted the stiff, lifeless body into his arms.

"We are but a small company," Will Shipman was saying afterward in the dryness of the inn, "servants of Lord Crowley. We were the Children of Bristol, though but one among us is—or was—a boy. We played in Bristol and in Exeter and in London, hanging by the skin of our teeth and living poorly, sleeping where we might and playing for anyone who would serve us meat and drink. I can mend shoes, pick pockets, or sing a naughty ballad. I was a scholar once, but acting is what I do best."

"And the boy?" Matthew interrupted, seeing the man's mind was beginning to wander.

"He joined us in Bristol. A runaway 'prentice, I suspect, though he never said but that he had an uncle in Lincoln by whom he stood in the way of an inheritance in not too many years. We took him on as costume boy, but about that time our "lady," James Fitzhue, took sick and died, so we gave Richard James's part. The lad had a natural way with words. In a woman's garb you could not tell him from a queen's maid. He did his work with the company, paid his way. His Dido made the play; and that was what, I'm sure of it, got us invited to perform before Sir Henry Saltmarsh at the Hall, although I suspect that's off now."

"Sir Henry came to see you play at the inn?"

"No, he had seen us at Bristol in April last, had even given us money for lodgings and other expenses. He asked us who the boy was, said he had seen worse at the Globe and that the lad had a future if he knew how to make the most of it. I did not try to stop Richard, though good boy players are hard to come by these days."

"Did the boy have enemies?"

"Enemies?" The ruddy-faced man snorted contemptuously. "Why, a sweeter lad you would not wish, though you had the making of him. There was none among us but loved him like a son or brother. He will be sorely missed, God rest him."

The man settled deeper into his melancholy, and seeing that there was no help for it, Matthew asked, "Where will you go now?"

"We were to play tonight at the Hall. If we are still welcome, Samuel Peacham will play Dido. God help us that his voice does not break, for he's nearer thirty than eighteen, though he has but half a beard. . . .

"There was none among us but loved him like a son or brother," the big player repeated, more to himself than to the clothier. "Whoever did it, he was a devil—or she. Though I doubt that a woman could have done him so, not Richard."

"Pray God no," Matthew Stock said, straightening his hat. "Did you find the body?"

"The girl found him. I heard her scream and woke from a sound sleep to find her bending over him weeping."

Matthew thought of the slender dark-haired girl with the pale face and sorrowful eyes who had brought his ale, and he thought of Richard Mull's poor outraged corpse half buried in the straw, and where it lay now in the cart ready to be drawn to the churchyard.

"Did she know him, I mean before?"

"No more than did we all," Will Shipman replied after a moment's hesitation. "She waited tables at the inn, and once or twice joined in the singing. I think she was there at one giving of the play, a poor one that, with no more than a drunken furrier and his haughty dame and a pair of spindly-leg scholars down from Cambridge as lookers-on. The innkeeper treats her wretchedly. He tolerates us here as a finch the lark, only to have someone from whom he might snatch more than he deserves. We pay dearly for his filthy straw and bad meat."

"Why then did you not leave?" Matthew asked.

" 'Twas as I have said, where might we have gone? Larger and better companies revel in London, such as we must rest content with their leavings. So we are here at the sufferance of Sir Henry and his lady."

The fire had died and the room was as cold as church on Monday and as empty. Will Shipman called for more drink, and from the back of the tavern the girl came, her face full of grief. Will Shipman called for a fire and ale. She picked up logs and placed them on the grate. Presently the fire revived and was filling the room with its warmth. Then she fetched the drink, and Matthew noticed for the first time that she was comely, with fine features, buxom, and on the verge of womanhood. He started to speak but then thought the better of it. She was young; she had found the body; her vacant stare and pale lips told him of her mind.

Matthew looked up to see Sir Henry's secretary enter the tavern. Outside it was still raining, a cold, cheerless drizzle. Varnell greeted the two men and sat down at their table.

"We meet again, Master Stock," Varnell said; then he addressed the chief player: "Will Shipman, my message is for you."

Will Shipman, who had hardly seemed to notice the secretary's entrance, looked up grimly. Matthew observed at once that there was little love between the two men.

"Sir Henry will have the play as was arranged. Tonight at the Hall, the boy's murder notwithstanding."

"Never fear," Will Shipman replied. "We'll serve his pleasure."

Varnell looked about the room with obvious distaste, then back at the player. "My mistress dislikes bawdry. See that there is no foul matter in the play. What is it that you perform?"

"Dido, Queen of Carthage."

"An old play, then," the secretary replied with a smirk. "By Kit Marlowe I believe."

"If you know the play then, you know as well that there's no offense in it."

"There are many ways to offend, Master Shipman, many," the secretary remarked casually, looking about him again.

Will Shipman grunted.

"Well, then, our business is quickly done." Varnell said with evident satisfaction. The player finished his ale at a gulp, saluted Matthew and the secretary brusquely, and strode out into the yard. Varnell looked at Matthew. "I'm glad to see you about your constableship. These players keep close counsel. I would be very much surprised if he that has just left would tell you aught but how to hang yourself in a hurry." The secretary laughed at his own joke. "Have you found out anything?"

"Something of their lot, and of the boy's. But if you mean have I yet tracked the murderer I am sorry to say no."

"No clues?"

"Not a one," Matthew said, shaking his head.

Varnell rose and asked, "Richard Mull—his body is already buried?"

"I think the players see to that work now."

"A pity, the boy's death. He was so young. A miserable morning for a burial too. The grave will fill with water before Richard Mull is in it."

"He is beyond such worries now," Matthew reflected, finishing his ale and making a move to rise.

The secretary's eyes narrowed. "I see that you are a philosopher as well as a clothier and constable."

"Not a philosopher, sir," Matthew replied firmly, "nought but a clothier by trade and constable by vote of my neighbors, and that but for a year with but three months to run."

"Let us pray, then," Varnell said, "that it does not take you the remainder of your term to find out Richard Mull's murderer."

Matthew felt the sting of the rebuke but said nothing. The secretary walked toward the door, though he looked back once as though to add a word. When he was alone, Matthew watched the fire until it began to die again, then he left the payment for his ale upon the table, found his cloak where he had left it near the door, and stepped into the innyard. The rain had stopped, but he knew the road would be a sea of mud. Across the innyard Will Shipman and three other men were hitching a horse to a cart wherein the body of Richard Mull lay. Matthew waited until the chief player mounted the cart and took the reins. The little group nodded to him as they passed, and Matthew removed his hat.

When they had passed, he pulled his cloak tightly around him, replaced his hat firmly on his head, and made his way back to the high road, careful of his footing in the soft, moist earth.

The walk homeward was longer and harder than the journey out, and the thought of his commission weighed heavily upon him. When nominated for constable, he had been pleased and honored, happy in the thought that the office might lead to something greater. He saw himself perhaps as alderman, or even mayor. Now he realized the office was no mere sinecure. The boy was dead, brutally and inexplicably so. His violated body would soon rest in the churchyard, his golden voice still, swallowed in that awesome silence that stills at last all voices, while his murderer doubtless somewhere called for meat and drink, picked fleas from his beard, or roasted his feet by a cheery fire. The boy must have justice, Matthew Stock resolved as he trudged through the mud, careful to avoid the holes and ruts filled with faggots and brushwood.

3

*T*HEY were quarreling again, perhaps about the boy. The secretary lingered near the heavy oak door longer than he would normally have deemed politic, trying to make something of the murmur of voices beyond, but he picked up only the tone of the quarrel, not its substance. Twice he heard the word "London," and once, uttered with the violence of an oath, the word "coach." Then footfalls caused him to draw quickly from the door and hurry down the gallery toward his own chamber.

His lodgings were simply furnished. There was the bed and chest, a small desk on which he placed his writing materials, and the few books he had brought from Cambridge but had not opened since. A window gave out onto a small garden. Upon his desk was a stack of his employer's letters nearly ready for the London post, and a legal document which he now sat down to recopy in a thin but elegant Italian script.

Since the copying was effortless, it was not long before Varnell was caught up in a reverie of the sort in which he especially enjoyed indulging. He saw himself in London at some great man's house, but not as a mere secretary. He was rather one to whom others paid deference. There were ladies present, of course. One, particularly beautiful, had come to his master for a request. But first she must pass through him, him without whom no one sees, much less speaks to, his lordship. She is pleading, she begins to weep, her hair falls long and golden to her alabaster shoulders and she looks up respectfully, submissively, while he, with his face half turned away and his eyelids nearly closed, brushes lint from a new satin suit.

The fantasy is revised, and as the secretary begins the second page of the document the scene shifts to a place he knows well. It is a public house, somewhat decayed, its sign that of the Owl. The mistress of the house is a thick-waisted robust woman with frizzled gray hair and a face the two sides of which seem at war with each other. He cannot recall her name; he does not try, for she is stupid and her breath reeks of garlic and her breasts hang heavy beneath a wine-stained smock. Another woman graces his imagination as he copies. She is young, slender as a boy, with full lips and eyes the color of the sea. For her he must pay the fat woman five shillings. He remembers particularly because it is all that he has in his purse, and she allows him to take the girl upstairs only after he has paid her price. The stairway is dark and foul-smelling, the bed-chamber cold and filthy with litter. The girl huddles in a corner like a child, her eyes round with fright. He beckons her to come; she hesitates. Finally he grabs her by the wrists, surprised at her strength. They struggle and he places his hand over her nose and mouth until she yields, whimpering like a dog. He is drenched with sweat from the struggle.

Now, however, he shivered, for the small fire in the grate was not enough to warm the corner where his desk stood. He rose from his place and paced to warm his feet and limbs, catching a glimpse of himself in the mirror he used when he shaved himself every third day. His skin was mottled, but discreetly powdered; his teeth were unusually good. He turned up his thick lips to appreciate the effect. The teeth were white and straight; not two lords in three had the like, and he the second son of a cobbler of Corn-wall.

The thought invited another series of recollections. The scene is Cambridge in the chamber he shares with Wilfred, the son of a bareboned knight of Cornwall with an allowance of a pound a week and not the sense of an ass. Wilfred says that divinity is for beggars who prefer the bishops' crumbs to the meat of the lords temporal. Wilfred is making plans to go down to London and the Inns of Court, where he will study the law, the only avenue to preferment, he argues. Let the young simpleton go and spend his father's money on whores and penny ballads and plays. Ah, yes, plays, which Wilfred learns by heart, for he is also of a literary turn of mind.

The plays make Peter think of Will Shipman, whom he detests. The man is always grinning wryly from that monstrous growth of hair upon his chin. No man is such a fool as he who does not know that he is dirt, who cannot be civil to those whom God has made his superiors in worth as well as in station. Yet Sir Henry feasts the players in London while the secretary sits at table's end, his face firmly set in deference to the knight and his lady he serves, while the bumpkin player, full to the brim of his cups, leans across the table on his great hairy elbows as though he were in a common tavern.

The girl struggled, he remembered. He was wet with sweat, but his strength was greater than hers. When she surrendered, she lay there like an effigy on a tomb.

It would be winter in two months' time. They would return to London and, as a reward for his service to them both, they would take him with them. He would have a finer chamber than this, its walls to be hung for warmth and perhaps beauty; Sir Henry would entertain as befitted his station; Peter Varnell would occupy a higher seat at table, and who could tell? His service becoming known among those with influence at court, he might live still to tutor a prince, or win distinction in some even greater way.

He had ripped her ragged smock. She scarcely moved; the devil take her.

Once in London during the holidays he had heard a famous preacher discourse upon the text: "How long shall the wicked triumph?" Yes, that was it. He had not remained at Cambridge, but he had learned his divinity. Let Will Shipman, as the boy had done, capture her ladyship's roving eye, let him exult in his privileges with Saltmarsh. The corn must grow green before it is cut. Saltmarsh would know who served him best.

Peter Varnell resumed copying, the little exercise having warmed his feet. At an hour's end his work was done; he held several pages up to the light of the window, both to note possible errors and to admire the perfection of his craft. He replaced the quill in its stand and walked into the gallery, surrounded on all sides by gloomy portraiture of his employer's forebears gazing on in dumb disapproval. At the door of the study he paused, as though to examine a portrait on the opposing wall. He heard nothing within. They had gone, he supposed.

"As yet you have said nothing." She spoke sharply, bitterly, erect of back as though posing for the artist's brush.

"The boy is dead. He is even now buried in the churchyard. I have charged the constable. What more would you have?"

She detested these measured phrases of her husband's, the cutting edge of his superiority. She responded calmly, "I would have you tell me by whose hand this thing was done."

"That is Master Stock's business to discover. As magistrate, I have commissioned him. Why can that not suffice you?"

She sat down in the large Italian chair he had had made for himself in Florence. "So you have," she said cuttingly, attempting at the same time to match his composure. "Oh, you do follow the courses of the law like an obedient hound when it serves your purpose. Master Stock is witless and dull like the rest of the town, and will find nought more than his hat in his hand. Had you been concerned with the boy's murder, you would have pursued the matter yourself. Instead, you chose a man who can do little more than officiate at a bread pudding."

"He is much respected in the town," her husband replied evenly.

"Which means," she continued, "that he is prince among bumpkins, for I would not give you a farthing for the lot of them. Oh, I am sick to death of this place."

She rose and began to pace the floor. She hated him when he was thus, so full of himself.

"You had interests here yourself, did you not?"

The question having caught her when her back was turned, she was uncertain of its tone and did not answer until she could look at him squarely. Even then, his heavy features were a mask of ambiguities. "I am, sir," she began dryly, "interested in my husband's health and happiness, in the proper management of his household. I believe, as you well know, it may be truly said that in all things I have been most obedient."

This last phrase she uttered with peculiar emphasis. He looked up, and for a moment she thought she saw his lips twitch in anger.

"You had your own pleasures," he said, suppressing a yawn.

Before replying she examined the familiar face, the broad forehead, the brown and leathery skin of one who seemed to spend all his days in the sun, the heavy lines around eyes almost too small in company with his other features, and most prominent of all, the unusually thick lips. "Yes, I have had my pleasures," she replied calmly, "and yet they have been nothing less than the foundation of your own. Have I done aught that you would have had differently?"

When he responded, it was to a different question, but she was accustomed to his shifting of the grounds of their disputes. "I have my own interests, my needs, as does any man. Since I have provided well enough for you, I should not think you would have aught to complain of. Your father was poor enough."

"I am hardly the better now," she said scornfully. "You have probed that wound too often for it to bleed again. Besides, you were well, husband, to look to your own affairs. Were it not your wish to avoid your creditors we might be in London still. That we remain in the provinces now is a wonder to our friends as much as it is a horror to me.''

"We remain here because London is unhealthy," he replied defensively.

"Unhealthy for you, you mean," she said.

"And for you as well, my dear. After all, sickness does not spare the virtuous, you know."

"I wonder then that it has spared you, even here." With that, she walked to the window.

"If you can no longer tolerate me, you may take the coach to London," he said.

"The common coach? Are you mad?"

"Our coach. I will have Edwards drive you. You may proceed to London at your leisure."

"That gloomy, insolent fellow. I would prefer to drive the horses myself."

"You may do as you choose."

"Your gallantry is overwhelming," she said.

"It is invited by your modesty and goodhousewifery," he replied, his lips twisted ironically.

"Henry?" she began.

"Yes?"

"You shall not put me off about the boy, you know."

He made a gesture of silence at his lips and walked toward the door. In the gallery beyond he could hear fading footsteps. Husband and wife glared at each other, their expressions fixed in implacable hatred.

"Do you really trust that man?" she asked.

"Implicitly," he replied. "Master Varnell wants nothing so much in life as to climb upon my back to another lord's service. I cannot but trust such single-minded ambition in one so devoid of qualities. Besides, I must forgive his curiosity about our affairs if he is to be my factor in my curiosity about others."

"Do you not mean mine?"

He smiled coldly. "Perhaps so, yet Varnell's long nose will prove as useful to me in London as it has here, never fear."

She sneered and paced again impatiently. "You think

yourself clever. Do not prove excessively so. Perhaps the clothier will do your work after all. Since you have so able a tool in Master Varnell, you may find yourself undone in Master Stock. I would not find the irony of such an outcome unpleasing.''

He laughed but without conviction. ''I am surprised to hear you say so, having within the half hour so rudely bespoken our friend the constable. But rest assured, I do not employ tools I cannot wield. Master Varnell shall do what I will, as shall Master Stock.''

She detested his continual self-assurance. She said, ''And what have you promised the constable that he fly so willingly to your lure?''

''The constable? Why he is quite a different bird, his flaw being not in desiring to be more than he is but in being so unremittingly what he is—an honest man. He is more predictable than the sun. A man may set time by him.''

''Was Richard Mull also your tool?''

''No more than he was yours, lady. But let that rest. The boy is dead, and if you can suffer me these five days we shall proceed to London. Would that please you?''

''It would please me to go to London, even with you,'' she said, defeated.

''Very well, then. Tonight we shall have Master Shipman and his company as we originally purposed. I am minded to some tragic theme, and the suffering of Dido will do well enough.''

They fell into a grim silence; he warmed his hands at the fire in the hearth. She gazed from the window to the garden. Then she turned and looked at him steadily.

He said nonchalantly, ''Pray look that cook prepares enough for the players. They eat heartily.''

''I know my duties,'' she replied, closing the door firmly behind her.

The girl unmanned him, the devil take her. He caressed her, but it was as though he were trying to bring a frozen corpse to life. He could do nothing but weep from exhaustion and frustration. The hag of the tavern pounded upon the door. ''Pray be less noisy,'' she had screeched with a

25

voice like a whip across a beggar's back. "I keep an honest house and will have no riot." He had lain on the bed weeping. The girl had unmanned him, the devil take her. Rub salt into her pale cheeks, pale as death, until they glow like hellfire and she awakens to my desire.

But she had not awakened. She lay staring into the rafters while he had struggled in the darkness for his garments. Later he had listened at the door for her breathing, her weeping, but there had been nothing, nothing but silence from within and the murmurs of another's passion in the chamber beyond.

Once in London he had seen an earl's coach run down a child in the street. A crowd had quickly gathered around the broken body. He had remembered vividly the lord's face at the window: a handsome youthful face with but the trace of a beard at the chin and hair at the upper lip soft as down and almost as light as the young earl's face. The young lord had worn a Spanish cape, Peter Varnell remembered. He wished he might have such a one. The coach did not stop; the young lord did not stop. Peter Varnell had not stopped either, would not have stopped, had rode on through the darkening streets lulled by the clatter of hooves on cobblestones and the raw shouts of the driver and the mute curses of the folk as they stared enviously from their doorways and called their brats in from the twisted, narrow streets.

He would not have stopped then, but at this moment he did to rest at the top of a rise from which he might see the Hall, its outbuildings, and the fields beyond. The rocky surface of the hillock was dry, but he removed his cloak and placed it beneath him and stretched his long legs out before him. For the while it took him to catch his breath, he watched an ant ply the length of his boot before shaking it off into the thin brown grass. On such days as this, his mind full of images of desire, he had walked into the countryside around Cambridge, away from his dreary chamber at the college where he was regularly the butt of jokes about his poverty and Cornish accent. He had aspired to the church, but had fallen from grace the first year at the university, half seduced by the blasphemous Wilfred, half

26

by his own natural inclination for experiences of a more vivid nature than permitted by the cassock. He would have repented had his fall come a year earlier, but by the third year at Cambridge he felt himself quite beyond redemption. Wilfred, an eager reader of the more fashionable Italian authors, had helped to convince him that true felicity lay in getting a secure place in some great lord's affairs, and since attaining his degree he had been busily engaged in that cause.

For the people of the town he had nothing but contempt, although his own social origins were no grander, but as he viewed it himself, his degree, if nothing else, proved him their better. His enthusiasm for London, the only city of the realm worthy the name, was matched only by that for his lady, Cecilia Saltmarsh, whose high forehead, pencil brows, thin lips, and bodily form the delicious contours of which were merely suggested in the elegant lines of her gowns, represented to him all he knew of sensual delight. What pleasure he should have taken in being more to her than her husband's servant; and the truth was that he lived in hope of seeing himself something more to her than a mere household furnishing. Did she think of him at all? Did she see him at all as daily he executed his employer's affairs in the great house? He studied to deserve more than her praise of him.

And that had been precisely what had vexed him about the boy: that at a time when his own presence in the house might have become increasingly conspicuous and his worth noted, a pasty-faced actor with but three hairs on his chin should have had more attention from his mistress than he himself had garnered in three months' service. But his mistress was fascinated by plays—and players. He could not himself abide them. But all that was done now, since the boy was dead.

He rose to his feet, his long legs having gone stiff. Above, the clouds were again heavy with rain. He wrapped his cloak around him and started to walk back to the Hall. He trusted in his luck; it was a good half hour's walk and he was not altogether sure the new storm would allow him that.

27

Cecilia Saltmarsh was the only daughter of a Devonshire knight whose wife had died in childbirth and whose estate and morals had both declined under the high cost of London living. She had married Henry Saltmarsh shortly before her father's complete financial collapse. Her husband had generously paid the old knight's debts; but since he had immediately contracted new ones, Henry Saltmarsh's charity was to no avail. This good turn, however, her husband rarely allowed her to forget for more than a week at a time. The first few years of their married life they lived in a spacious house in a fashionable quarter of London and on an income from the Saltmarsh properties. This had allowed her to keep a lavish table and to save two dressmakers from the curse of idleness. She loved the theater, and when in London she had attended, with or without her husband, twice weekly, either at Mr. Henslowe's Rose or at the more intimate and prestigious Blackfriars. She was also fond of players, especially the young boys who took the women's parts, an interest her husband did not discourage. Saltmarsh had curious interests of his own. At first these had horrified and disgusted her; later she learned tolerance, and now both the knight and his lady had settled down to a tempestuous domesticity based on the principle that neither was to inquire too closely into the other's conduct.

The closet she examined at the moment was large but full, although she had brought but a sample from the house in London and of those only the gowns suitable for the season. She stood, her long slender arms akimbo, trying to make up her mind. Since she was especially proud of her fair skin, she chose a color to set it off to best advantage, handing the garment to Gwen, a pretty Welsh girl of fourteen who had been her maid for two years.

The girl took the gown and submissively laid it out on the purple coverlet of the bed.

"No," Cecilia Saltmarsh said imperiously, "not there. Into the antechamber. I will rest now. See that no one disturbs me for this hour."

The girl nodded and hurried from the room, careful that the gown not drag.

Cecilia Saltmarsh lay down on the bed, staring moodily up at the underside of a canopy painted ornately with moon and stars. The memory of her conversation with her husband vexed her still. Henry always vexed her, and she was certain he was lying about the boy. She always knew when he lied, but her knowledge never made his motives less enigmatic. Now she was determined to know the truth, not for truth's sake but because she took the boy's murder as a personal affront.

She was unable to sleep and soon gave up the attempt. She called for the Welsh girl, told her to find Varnell, and began to dress hurriedly. She did not like her husband's secretary. The man was ill-favored and mean, a scrambling man who would make any door an opportunity for his ambition. His attentiveness to her—yes, she had noted that and had sometimes averted her face to hide her laugher— had grown stale, had become insulting in its presumption of social equality. She had tolerated it only for amusement's sake and out of a simple curiosity to see how far he might go. Her father would have never endured such a scarecrow scholar in his service. She knew, however, her husband used the man for more than his secretary. That was Henry's way. She had no doubt Varnell was involved in her husband's present business with the players.

When he entered a few minutes later, Varnell bowed stiffly from the waist, his face pale with what she surmised was suppressed passion. She directed him to sit, asked if he were well in body and how he bore the recent cooler weather, and came to her point.

"I have a favor," she said.

"Lady?"

" 'Tis no great thing."

Varnell protested. He would do anything. She had only to speak it.

"My husband has told me of Richard Mull's murder. I am most sorry for it."

The secretary mumbled sympathetically beneath his breath, staring on boldly, not looking away as she had almost expected. She wondered if his brave face were innocence or merely his fascination with her, and decided it was the latter. "I am told the constable has been set on the murderer, whoever he may be."

"He has, and reports to Sir Henry this very day."

"When he does," she said. "I would know his report."

Varnell dropped his gaze at that and stood stiffly before her.

"Would that trouble you—conveying my husband's business to me? 'Tis more than a woman's curiosity. You know what favors we showed the boy," she said, wondering the while if the man really did and if so, in what coin her husband might have purchased his complicity. She repeated: "Were you to covey to me in confidence what you have either from my husband or from Master Stock you would do me a service I would not soon forget." She put the request sweetly now, so that it would hardly seem to admit a negative response.

Varnell looked confused. "I would be loath to tell of what passes within your husband's chambers. He is my employer and—"

"Come, come, Master Varnell. We are husband and wife. My husband's business is mine, and mine his. 'Tis as simple as that. Take heart. Such qualms as these are mere foolishness, like a maiden's blush. Sir Henry keeps from me only to spare my feelings, which I think at times he holds at too great account. I *would* know his mind."

She leaned forward so that he might appreciate the generosity of her rounded shoulders. Varnell sighed heavily, his face brightening with resolve. "You will find me your good servant," he said finally.

She smiled in triumph and rose. The chamber was drafty and she pulled a shawl close about her shoulders as she conducted the secretary to the door and watched him make his way down the long hall. A curious little man, she thought.

She leans toward him, her loose gown opening to the waist so that he can see her bosom, and smiles radiantly. He sits manly and erect and says, "I hope, lady, that I may have your complete confidence. It is no little thing you ask of me. Sir Henry is my master and I his servant, at least in the capacity of secretary, although my university training has prepared me for—''

A knock at his door shattered the scene, but Varnell made a note to himself to continue recalling it at his leisure. First discomfited by his interview with Cecilia Saltmarsh, he now found it most satisfying to remember. His prospects in the house, he decided, had never been brighter. He opened the door. It was the Welsh girl to tell him that Sir Henry wished to see him at once. Varnell sent the girl off pausing to inspect himself in the glass. He smoothed the blond hairs upon his upper lip and framed a politic countenance. The effect was right; the secretary was ready.

The two men sat facing each other over a glass of wine. Saltmarsh looked grim. ''When Master Stock comes with his tale I want you here too. Observe the man's manner and expression. Watch the eyes, especially the eyes. He may tell us less than he knows. 'Tis likely he'll be direct and unsuspecting but there's always the ill luck he may have discovered something. Some trifle overlooked in the enterprise.''

Saltmarsh paused and leaned forward in his chair. The spectre of ill luck hovered above Varnell's head threateningly. He realized his hands were trembling. ''I was most careful in all,'' he protested.

''The hostler will keep silent?''

''As death. I paid him well. The man's a scoundrel but he knows what's good for him. He'll say nothing.''

''Not even to save his own neck?''

Varnell had not considered that. He shifted uneasily in his chair. ''It would be his death as well,'' he reasoned.

Saltmarsh looked at him skeptically. ''And *yours*.''

Varnell wanted to say: ''And yours *too*, Sir Henry.'' But he didn't dare. He dropped his eyes. He heard his employer make a move to stand, and he rushed to his feet. He felt sick at heart and his vision blurred, but not from wine.

His employer took his arm and led him from the chamber smiling coldly. ''I'm sure you have nothing to fear,

Master Varnell. I have long admired your craft. Meticulous. I would be amazed were you not to show the same skill in your other duties. How much is it I pay you?''

In a weak, trembling voice Varnell named the sum.

"Well," Saltmarsh replied, jovially now. "It will be more—and in not a month's time. Hold me to it."

4

Matthew warmed himself by the kitchen fire, eating goat cheese and brown bread heavy with butter and honey.

"He had no enemies," he said between mouthfuls. "Others in the company liked him, if Will Shipman say true. Lady Saltmarsh encouraged him to try his fortune in London. He had no money; his people were poor, decent folk of Devonshire, who no doubt believe him alive still."

"Yet someone wished him dead," Joan said without looking up from her stitchery.

He paused to cut himself another sliver of the rich cheese. "Indeed, and not only dead but painfully done. 'Twas more than the snuffing out of a life."

"God comfort his parents in their grief when they come to know of it."

"Aye," he said.

"I suppose," she said, looking up from her work now to stare into the little licks of fire, "it comes of how they live, traveling from one place to the next, sleeping however they may. And for a boy to travel in such company."

"He was fourteen," Matthew said.

" 'Tis young enough," she said firmly. "Fourteen is fourteen, and that's far enough from twenty and a fuller knowing of life. For a woman 'tis different. Woman knowledge grows inside, like the sap in a tree. A man must learn of what is about him, but a woman knows already when she becomes a woman.''

They contemplated this mystery together, neither willing to interrupt the other's thought. The fire died out. Matthew finished the last crust of bread and rose to his feet.

"Must you go again?" she asked.

"I must, if only to tell Sir Henry I have found out nothing. The town might have found a better man to stand as constable this year.''

"And a worse," she replied with a smile of encouragement.

"Aye, but I seem to have come upon a closed door in this business. Men murder for some reason. They do it because they want what another man has, or because they hate what he has done, or what he is. Richard Mull, it would appear, had no more than he should. Yet he is dead. There is no clue to all of this, and soon I must to Sir Henry and say as much. 'Tis unlikely 'twill please him, since he himself bears his own office freshly.''

"Aye, and I wonder at that," she said. "And he one who spends more time in London than here. They might have chosen for Justice of the Peace one local in fact.''

"Well, his blood is good enough.''

"And his purse full enough," she returned quickly, "though he may plumb its depths sooner than he thinks.''

"He may indeed," her husband responded, "yet that is not for us to judge.''

She looked up from her work and smiled wryly. "My good Master Stock. I know I gossip overmuch, and beg your pardon and Sir Henry's too, though you cannot deny that I speak truth.''

He smiled. "I have never heard you speak aught but the truth, Joan. For all your gossip, I have never found you anything but truthful. If your husband is better at trade than as constable, 'tis no fault of yours.''

He started to go, but she stopped him. She said thoughtfully, " 'Tis possible you have found no reason for this murder because you suppose all men such as yourself, content with their lot, of a loving nature, and with reasons for what they do as ready as pennies in a purse. Some men act without reason, without thought. My father had a serving girl once who afterward killed a lad in the cornfield. They found her sitting by the boy's body, his throat cut neatly as though she were opening the belly of a pig. When the watch found her and asked her wherefore she had done the murder, she blamed the act on the slant of light upon the corn."

He said, "She was not in her right mind."

"Perhaps not, and yet later at her hanging she seemed calm and reasoned, begged those around about to take from her example, and before she died prayed to God for her soul. It made me weep to hear of it, for her voice was full of sadness and her face as lovely as a young child's. As she died, I turned my head suddenly, so that I would not have to see her death. It seemed almost to me as wrong as her murder of the young man was."

"I hope you doubt not that it was rightfully done."

"Not a whit," she replied in the same wistful tone of her story, "but 'twas how I felt. Sometimes a person cannot find a word for a feeling, nor explain it to another. It was simply there inside of me, not to be denied even if it could not be spoken."

He considered this, stroking the bristles on his cheek and looking down on his wife in her chair, her hands immobile in her apron, firelight playing on her oval face, quite lost in her thoughts. He said, "Yet I think somewhere there must be a reason."

"Think so still. As for me, I know there be things for which there are no reasons. God alone can comprehend them."

The girl pulled up her smock so that her calves were bare and touched the cold surface of the pond just enough to send green mossy waves in ever-widening circles. This effect she watched for some time as though compelled.

The trees about the pond formed a little grove out of sight of the inn. She stepped farther into the water; it climbed up to her knees. She held up her smock even higher, an immodesty that only the privacy of the place and her present state of mind permitted. Her feet, ankles, and calves numbed, as though they were not a part of her. She stepped farther; the water came to her thighs and took her breath away, and still she walked, her feet sinking now into the ooze at the pond's bottom. Then she stopped and waited until her mind's eye had found its place in her memory.

At first Richard had not noticed her among the servants, but she had seen him. He had been caught up in his part and spoke with a voice different from his own. She reasoned that he did not speak for himself but according to what the playwright disposed. That was why Dido did not look at her, but at the other player, at Aeneas, not where he wished to cast his eye but at where the play required. But when the play was done and Richard Mull had cast off his woman's garb, would he see her then?

He did look at her later. She felt him watching her as the players drank and called for meat. The hour was late and she was weary with serving, for her day began early. His flaxen hair and pale skin were more beautiful than Dido's. He spoke and lifted his cup, inviting her to drink with him. She accepted, and when the master looked away she drank from his own cup, the cup his own lips touched. They had tasted each other's lips that way. Standing in the water reaching up to her thighs, she experienced the joy of it again.

The wind caused the water to ripple, the trees to bend in response, and she returned to herself and the present, standing in the pond like a statue in a rich man's garden. But then the picture returned.

After the play they drank, they all drank until the merchant and his fat wife were locked in each other's arms in the corner fast asleep and Big Tod and Little Tod sang quietly some plaintive song from their own country. She and Richard sat at the table alone, for Will Shipman had fallen asleep upon the board. She was not used to drink and her head ached. Richard stared into the fire as though watching a little play amidst the great logs and bright tongues of flame. After a while he rose and led her from the room and into the night.

The master was not about to order her to the scullery or to bed, so she and Richard walked silently together, hand in hand, toward the stable. Suddenly out of the darkness a man had come. He had beckoned to Richard. His cloak was thick like the coat of a bear and she could not make out his features, only the sound of his voice, which was low. He and Richard whispered together briefly, words that she could not decipher, and then Richard turned to her, took her face in his hands, and kissed her so gently that she hardly felt the touch upon her lips. Then he was off into the night, unaccountably, and her heart was full of joy.

She no longer felt the cold; she was hardly conscious of her body at all, a loose, fleshly, insubstantial thing hanging about her. Boldly she stepped farther, pulling her smock over her head.

The hostler sat on the ground picking fleas from his beard, his legs crossed. He muttered resentfully, "You're the constable, are you?"

"Then you know I have power to make my word good."

"I'll tell you that the boy thought himself to be a fine bird. 'Tis no wonder someone wearied of him and plucked his feathers."

"You did the deed yourself, did you?" Matthew put his question sharply, thinking to take the man by surprise.

"If I did, would I be talking as I be now, bragging? I am no fool." The hostler groveled in the straw as though anticipating a blow.

Matthew changed his tack. "Where was the boy last night when you saw him last?"

"The lot of them drank themselves to sleep. I watched them from the window."

"You watched them? Why?"

The hostler spit in the dirt. "Why to see them, man. Dost think I prefer the company of horses because I live in the stable? I watched them all from the window as they one by one fell into sleep or went their own ways."

"Who went his own way and where?" Matthew asked with interest.

37

"The merchant and his wife huddled in the corner like merry kittens. The players were strewn hither and yon upon the tables."

"And where was your master while all this was going on?"

The hostler spit upon the ground and uttered a curse. "He was looking to his own business, that's what; and if you must know, then you might ask him yourself."

"I will," Matthew replied dryly, his irritation beginning to grow at the man's surliness. "And where was the boy Richard Mull?"

The hostler paused, fingered in the straw with his right hand as though looking for a lost object. "He was minding his business with one of the maids, and should that prick your interest you may ask of him further, though I doubt that he's mind to reply, his ears and mouth now stopped with dirt." The hostler emitted a dry laugh, hardly distinguishable from a cough.

"You know I can have you whipped?" the clothier said sternly.

"You find me insolent, as they say?"

"Where was the boy?" Matthew repeated.

The hostler laughed again. "He was with the girl, her with the lofty nose that's too good to look upon a poor man. They sat at the table—I saw them—sharing a cup. I knew his mind."

"And what was his mind?"

"Why to bed, o'course, and the sooner the better."

"And did he bed her?" Matthew asked.

The hostler began to rise. "You may ask her, for she would have had the pleasure of him, not me. I must look to my horses."

"I am not finished with you," Matthew said sharply, pushing the old man downward. "Did you see the girl and Richard Mull go off together?"

"Maybe," the hostler replied enigmatically. "I saw them leave, followed them across the courtyard. I watched them go their own ways in the darkness, she back to the kitchen where she belonged before the moon was up."

"Then Richard Mull left her?"

"How might I know that? Maybe they met somewhere in the dark. Such deeds are best done in the dark, so that the devil may see 'em and mark those that do such foully."

Matthew felt about in his purse; he found two coins, which he drew forth and held before the man's face.

"This may put you to sleep sweetly if you'll satisfy me as to the whereabouts of the boy."

The hostler's eyes lighted up with interest. "And how much would that be, sir?"

Matthew reached into his purse again and withdrew five more shillings. "This," he said, holding out his hand, "but only if you can find it in you to recall with whom Richard Mull went off and where."

Simon wrung his hands and coughed deeply. "I said he was with the girl and they went off into the dark together."

"So you say," Matthew replied curtly. "But that's not all that I've paid for."

Simon didn't answer directly. He hummed to himself and busied his hands with his hostler's tools. The man was thinking, and Matthew decided to wait.

"Well?" Matthew said, after a while.

The hostler stopped humming and looked up. "Were there as many coins again in my hand I might help you to a secret."

"How so?" asked Matthew.

"First, promise the other five shillings."

"Done," said Matthew, "but it must be worth the cost. Otherwise, you have no promise."

"There was another one last night," the hostler said. "Man or woman I could not tell. He, or she, beckoned to the boy and the lad followed. They didn't see me. I hid behind a bush, moved quiet and quick like a flea in a fine lady's farthingale."

"Where was this other one you speak of?"

Simon pointed to a stand of sturdy oaks on the other end of the pasture. "I followed them to know their business."

"Which was?" Matthew prompted.

The hostler shrugged. "The two of 'em talked. There was a pair of horses, too, tethered in the trees, I could hear the creatures snorting and stamping and see their shadows beneath the branches." The hostler held out his hand for payment. It was covered with filth, the fingers were contorted like a claw.

"Not so fast," Matthew said sharply. "What did the boy and this stranger do?"

"They talked. I couldn't hear. I left them to themselves and went to bed. The night was cold and I was shivering."

"You didn't see the horses?"

The hostler looked down thoughtfully. "Pitch black, that's what 'twas, and darker in the trees there. Each horse had four legs, but I can swear no more." Simon thrust his hand forward. Matthew handed him the coins reluctantly. The hostler murmured thanks and limped off across the yard, smiling to himself.

Matthew watched him go, wondering if he had been a fool to pay such a contemptuous fellow. It was not much of a story he had been told, but it was all the constable had and he was glad of it. A mysterious stranger and a pair of horses. Why two horses? he wondered, unless there were in fact two men, besides the boy, or perhaps the other horse was *for* the boy? He looked across the muddy pasture to the stand of oak and was about to proceed there when he thought the better of it. It was growing late, and he wanted to talk to the serving girl and to Will Shipman again before he paid a visit to the Hall.

He could not find the girl in the inn. The other scullery maids, Tabitha and May, had not seen her since midday. The innkeeper grumbled that her disappearance was not unusual, that such was the sad state of serving girls that they hardly did what they were paid to do before vanishing to do the devil's work.

"From her I have not had two day's work in as many years," Master Rowley fumed while pushing a tun of ale into its place. The big man was sweating fiercely. "If you find her, tell her she is no servant of mine unless she looks to her work better than she has done this past week."

In the yard Matthew found Will Shipman and the other players loading a wagon with the trappings of their craft, some bulky gowns and a painted tree, fully leafed in summer green. The players talked busily among themselves, and Matthew was of a mind to pass them by before Will Shipman hailed him. The chief player left the work to his friends and hurried over to the constable.

"A word, please, Master Constable?"

Matthew stopped and greeted the burly actor.

Will Shipman said, "If you should be seeing Sir Henry before we do at nightfall, would you tell him that we have found a replacement for the boy and that the play will be performed as we had promised?"

Matthew was in the middle of assuring the actor that the message would not be out of his way, since he would be seeing Sir Henry within the hour, when it occurred to him that, saving for the scullery girl, Will Shipman was as likely to know of Richard Mull's involvement with the Saltmarsh family as anyone. He drew the actor aside where their voices would not be heard.

"Master Shipman, can you tell me if at any time since your coming to town Richard Mull was entertained at the Hall?"

The big actor frowned, stroked his beard, and said, "We were all entertained there, and royally too, upon coming to this place four days ago. Sir Henry and his lady feasted us in the great hall and heard an old play we had done to some applause in Norwich. If there were other times when the boy came alone, I know them not, for although I was close to the boy as any, he was a quiet one, full of his own thoughts and not given to sharing them with others. But if you ask concerning his entertainment at Norwich," he continued after a moment's pause, "then I must give you a different answer, for when we arrived in that city her ladyship sent her maidservant to us at play's end to ask about the boy and he went with her, although I know not where. Later when he returned he would not tell us what passed, beyond the delicacies of the table and her hope that such a one as he might find better fortune. None of us wished him aught but well."

"She was his patroness, then?"

"Indeed," the actor replied. "She fed his belly and his fancy; thereafter he had a fine conceit of himself."

Matthew studied the actor's face. He could see no guile,

no jealousy, there. The man had a faraway look in his eyes, as though he were remembering something fondly. Will Shipman said, "It was all we could do to keep Richard in the bloom of girlhood. His voice was on the verge of changing. We had good times, in the towns and on the roads. He had a gentle nature, but he was fit and could walk ten miles before dinner without a complaint."

Matthew asked, "Did the lady ever send for the boy. I mean to come alone?"

The big actor paused before replying, "I think not," he said. "The time in Norwich we played in an inn, and Lady Saltmarsh's maidservant called for the boy and they walked off together. Sir Henry and his lady had a fine house not a mile from where we played. It would have been an easy walk for a one-legged man."

"I suppose Richard Mull was properly grateful for Lady Saltmarsh's attentions?"

"I do not doubt it," Will Shipman said.

"And that there was no jealousy among others in the company concerning those attentions."

The actor's face darkened. He said coldly, "I have said nay to that question afore. There's not one among us that would have wished the boy anything but good, even if it meant his leaving us for one of the great companies. Surely none among us wished him dead for any reason. Now if you will pardon me, I and my men must load our gear."

"It seems your fellows have done your work while we have talked," Matthew said, looking over the actor's shoulder to where Big Tod and Little Tod had just finished loading the wagon and were standing staring curiously in his direction.

"Nonetheless, I must be about my business, as you yours," Will Shipman said curtly.

"Indeed, we must. And you must know, Master Shipman, that it is my commission to discover the murderer of Richard Mull, and I trust you have no objection to it."

The actor lowered his eyes. "If you find the boy's murderer, you shall have a friend forever in Will Shipman, I promise you that. But do not say aught against the good faith of me or my men. We are honest, though we be players, and we live by God's laws.''

"I trust that you do," the constable said, smiling, eager to have their conversation end on a more friendly note.

The actor turned and walked to where his fellows stood waiting. By this time Simon had brought up a horse and was at work hitching it to the wagon. Matthew watched as the three actors led the horse toward the road.

The chill of the pond took her breath away, but only for a moment, and she resumed breathing more slowly. She took another step into the water, and all her muscles came alive as she lost her footing in the mossy bottom. Then she was under the water, her eyes squeezed shut, and the darkness passed over her like a cloud across the face of the moon.

Saltmarsh Hall was a square, stone house with two towers and many windows. It was surrounded by a gracious park, had a goodly garden and pasture, an orchard of quinces, apples, pears, and plums, and a porter's lodge at the gate house. Matthew stood at the park paling to catch his breath. He had since morning been twice to the Triple Crown, once in a steady rain, twice upon a muddy road. It had been the same road Will Kemp had danced over the year before, when that madcap fool had created a sensation by dancing a morris from London to Norwich. Matthew and Joan had been in the throng that had gone out to greet him at Widford Bridge. But that was Will Kemp. Matthew was not so nimble. He had walked for his health and to spare the mare's legs, but now he was tired and discouraged. He had spoken to Will Shipman, to the innkeeper, and to the hostler. He had inspected the scene of the crime and the body of the victim, but had nothing more to report to Saltmarsh than the hostler's tale of a fatal meeting in the dark, a stranger and a pair of horses. Matthew realized he knew nothing for sure but that the boy was dead. He had seen that himself, to his regret he thought as the image of the brutalized body floated up again into his awareness like the memory of an old sin.

* * *

Alice had brought news of the scullery maid while Joan was still sitting in the window watching her husband turn beyond the glover's and head up High Street.

"The poor dear thing," she said in response to the news. She searched among her store for an appropriate proverb and finding none, settled on a phrase of her own coinage: "One sad death wants company."

"It is too true," Alice said, nodding her head sagely and still breathless. "They found her floating face up in the pond, and the water as icy as death. Brenner brought her back wrapped in a blanket, light upon his shoulders as though she were nothing more than a sheaf of corn newly mowed."

Joan mused, "She died then by her own hand?"

"Aye, she did by all accounts, although I suppose the master will be looking into it, him constable."

"I suppose he will, worst luck for him."

She rose and placed her work on the shelf. "And now, since he will return in three hours' time, we must prepare supper and something hardy, for I trust that discovering the acts of wickedness is harder on an honest man's back than the making of cloth or the selling of it, no matter the quality."

Alice, as much as her cheerful rotundity would permit, scurried to the yard to slaughter a hen. Joan walked quietly to the window and for a few moments watched the passers-by, their bodies bent forward against the cold. She contemplated the life in the street in all of its color, variety, and, as she now reflected, vanity. She was given to such somber impulses, and in times such as now she preferred her own company, as much as she loved her husband. She had seen the dead girl from time to time; perhaps she might have distinguished her from others of her age at market or at church, but even as she thought of her the image began to fade like warm breath upon a glass. There remained but a vague impression of youth, vitality, and—even for one of such humble origins—the promise of something more, suddenly cut off—and by her own hand—in terrible violation

44

of God's canon against self-slaughter. It was a crime quite beyond her understanding.

The image of the players' boy erased that of the girl like an errant wind, and the brief juncture of the two inspired an idea. She made a note to discuss it with Matthew when he returned. She hoped he would not judge it too harshly.

The shop bell rang hectically. She hurried from the kitchen.

5

Matthew looked curiously about, waiting to be spoken to and not exactly sure what to do with his hands. The vast shadowy room was dominated by a massive writing table littered with papers, books, small statuary, coffers, and other objects the nature of which Matthew could not discern. The walls were paneled and hung with tapestries. The chairs, high-backed and ornately fashioned, were made, Matthew was sure, by no village carpenter. But what impressed him most were the books. They rose in shelves from floor to ceiling. Had he been told the room contained all the books written since Adam he would have believed it.

Henry Saltmarsh cleared his throat, which Matthew took as a signal to begin. To the left of the magistrate, Varnell looked on with amused contempt.

"I have made inquiries. Not all have proved fruitful."

"By which you mean, I hope," Saltmarsh said, "that *some* of your inquiries have borne fruit? Well, let us have a look at them. If they be good fruit, we shall not mind the quantity of them."

Matthew said, "I have spoken to the innkeeper and to

the chief of players, Master Shipman. The hostler at the inn told me a tale, though I know not how to credit it.''

''We will credit it or no,'' Varnell interrupted. ''Your duty is to report.''

''Keep silent, Master Varnell,'' Saltmarsh said sharply, his gaze fixed on the constable. The secretary's face blanched. ''You were about to tell us the hostler's tale,'' Saltmarsh said.

Matthew repeated the hostler's story, careful to omit no essential detail.

The knight and his secretary exchanged glances. ''The man could not say who the person was he saw or identify the horses?'' Saltmarsh asked when Matthew had done.

''He could not—or would not. He had concealed himself and watched only for a while. Then he went to bed.''

Saltmarsh heaved a sigh and looked into his lap. ''Then we know little indeed, Master Constable, and less, since as you say the man's story is somewhat lacking in credit.''

''I think I know the man, sir,'' Varnell added. '' 'Tis a hot day in December when he's sober.''

Saltmarsh said, ''I doubt it not, knowing the reputation of the Triple Crown. But have you not, Master Stock, something more—no suspects, no sturdy beggars lurking in the neighborhood who might have killed the boy for his purse?''

''None. But I am satisfied that the lad's companions are free of guilt. They seem honest, though players, and indeed were great lovers of the boy.''

''The innkeeper reported no quarrels among the players or travelers on the night of the murder?''

Matthew Stock said, ''He did not.''

''You are satisfied that the innkeeper speaks the truth?''

''He does, although I have no special liking for the man. He seemed most upset at the behavior of the scullery girl, who has not been seen since.''

''Might then she have part in this?''

''I know not. As I say, she has since disappeared. I suspect that the hostler tells us truthfully when he reports that she and the boy made merry together. It could be that she has run off, as such girls often do.''

"I would not then overlook her either, Master Stock. Have you spoken to all the players?"

"Only to Will Shipman."

"Then I advise you to speak to them all. Let your authority be known. Abide no insolence, for though they may have of me royal entertainment I shall endure no murders."

"I will look to this business as you have directed, sir."

The knight rose from his chair and extended his hand to Matthew, who, seeing the magistrate rise, made haste to do likewise.

"The players have prepared a little entertainment for us tonight, a tragic theme befitting this sad day. We have invited a few of the neighborhood—you must come, too, and bring your good wife with you. We will first eat and when the play is over and the players merry, you may notice something in their manner to suspect. I am not convinced yet that some jealousy among them is not at the root of this."

"You do us great honor—" Matthew protested, astonished by the invitation.

"Not at all," Saltmarsh replied firmly. "I hold you in high regard, Master Stock. The common good behooves us to see more of each other—and our wives as well. Your wife's name is Joan, is it not?"

The magistrate took Matthew by the arm and led him toward the door of the chamber. "Good day to you, Constable," the magistrate said almost cheerfully. "Pursue your commission, which I trust may bear richer fruit on your next visit."

Outside, Matthew looked back at the Hall with wonder and awe. He had given his account, poor thing that it was, and without apparent offense. Indeed, at his leaving, Saltmarsh had seemed most pleased with him. Matthew heaved a great sigh of relief and felt for the first time that day almost happy. Now as he walked his thoughts turned toward evening; he tried to imagine his wife's face when he told her the news. A play and supper too—at the Hall! He should not have been surprised had she refused to believe it or, taking him at his word, excused her three frayed gowns and worn cap—none of which she would feel would be fine enough for the occasion.

Once home, he broke the news to Joan and watched with astonishment as his little wife bounded up the stairs calling for Betty and Alice to lay out her best gown.

Varnell copied the document—a tedious bill of sale—with growing irritation and despair. All too suddenly had his employer brought him back to his own essential servitude in the house. Somewhere, he reflected bitterly, a great door had been shut on his expectations, and by nothing more than a word. The blockhead constable would in the end discover no more than he now knew, nothing. His commission was a jest, and why his employer could not see that too was more than the secretary could imagine. And this was he—the constable, damn him—whose silly speculations and idiot mutterings had been given a ready ear, while his own sound counsel so often went ignored. The constable would be given, no doubt, a high place at table—he and his wife, a dumpy wench, stale with child-bearing and barley bread. He had seen her once or twice scurrying after a fishmonger in the street for a supper of cod. The two of them would sit at a higher place than he! The thought galled him beyond endurance.

His one consolation now, now that the master had set other sail, was his mistress, who if she offered less promise of advancement, promised him in her eyes more immediate pleasures. The thought of it sustained him until supper.

Will Shipman balanced carefully on two legs of a stool. The actors had the inn to themselves, their host gone off to sleep or growl at his servants, but Will was in an ill-humor nonetheless. Samuel Peacham had shaved his face raw, as instructed, complaining all the while about loss of manhood, but his powdered jaws still betrayed the shadow of a beard.

"Lay on more paint, man," Will said. "And speak more slowly or you'll lose the wind of your treble and sound like a goat bleating for its mate."

Dressed in a long gown of purple, somewhat tattered

from use and musty from the chest, Samuel stopped in the midst of an expansive gesture of the right arm. "Damme, if I paint more, they'll think me my own ghost."

"And if less," Will retorted quickly, "a jaded sodomite and not the Queen of Love."

From the back of the room came a peal of hearty laughter, richly insolent.

"Let Aeneas come forward now," Will said with authority, ignoring the outcry from the back of the room.

Big Tod rose from where he had been seated enjoying Samuel Peacham's management of the new part and took several great strides to the center of the room, his arms akimbo. Without a pause he thundered, " 'Of Troy am I, Aeneas is my name; who driven by war from forth my native world, puts sails to sea to seek out Italy; and my divine descent from sceptered Jove: With twice twelve Phrygian ships I plow'd the deep, and made that way my mother Venus led; but of all them scarce seven do anchor safe, and they so wracked and weltered by the waves, as every tide tilts . . .' "

Big Tod played his part well, of that Will Shipman had no doubt. It was Samuel Peacham's performance that worried him. The voice was low and thin, and although his figure was slight enough for a woman's and his treble achieved moments of credibility, there was that about it which was so palpably false that he feared Dido's speeches might provoke more laughter than pity. The lad—Richard Mull—had had no peer at woman's roles. How Will missed him. The play was no great thing; it would now be the worse. Will's attention was drawn to Little Tod's ungainly Venus.

" 'Fortune hath favored thee, whate'er thou be, in sending thee unto this courteous coast. 'A' god's name on and haste thee to the court.' "

"By Christ," Big Tod exploded. "That's a wretched phrase, 'A' God's name on and haste thee to the court'!!" He mimicked the line in a high falsetto. "Why, he makes her sound an alewife."

"The lines are not mine, brother," Little Tod retorted sharply.

"The worst for that, for you could hardly have done less vilely."

Will was accustomed to this fraternal bickering, but he had little patience for it at the moment. He looked sternly at the larger of the brothers. "Silence," he shouted, his face reddening like a parboiled pig. "We have but one hour more to rehearse and then 'tis off to the Hall. Master Marlowe's play may not be to your liking, but 'tis what's wanted and what we shall provide. I'll have no more quarreling or baiting. Go on with your parts."

Little Tod continued, his brother stifling his impatience in a glare that made him an even more ferocious Aeneas than the play required. Will watched the scene disapprovingly, his face fixed in a scowl not at all typical of him. He was at the moment tired and hungry, and for this reason his humor was worn thin. He was also frightened; his company was at the end of its tether. With the death of the boy there would be less welcome at the Hall, or at any great house for that matter. While they might proceed to London in a week's time, there was no telling what success they would find. The future looked bleak.

He thought of the boy again, but now not so much to regret the lad's death as to consider the cause of it. He had told the constable less than he knew, almost more out of habit than a desire to keep certain facts to himself. He had learned in his years as an actor that between players and townsfolk a gulf was fixed and that even when there was great laughter or moving to tears, such an audience could have little love for the players, scorned and mistrusted as they were and classed with common thieves and sturdy beggars.

The truth was that he knew Richard Mull had occupied his place in the straw on but a few nights since their arrival in Chelmsford, that he did have "friends" other than his mates in the company, and that where there was such a division of interest there were indeed grounds of a quarrel. The girl at the inn had made great moon eyes at the boy, a look he remembered well himself how to read, although as a younger man he had taken quicker advantage of it. Richard had tickled the girl's fancy, and she was as plump and saucy as they came and certainly willing as a bitch in heat to 'scape the yard.

No, he thought, it must have had something to do with the other one, whosoever she was, that drew the lad out of nights. Had he got some girl with child and then threatened to run off? The boy was rootless, as were they all; he would never have allowed himself to be tied down to a green and swollen wench. And she, angered by his unwillingness, might have given him his deserts by probing his innards. Poor lad. Well, he thought, bringing the theme of his reflection to a conclusion while his company thundered on, let Matthew Stock untangle that skein, if he could. But Will doubted that, putting no faith whatsoever in constables or magistrates either. However it all came out, the boy was dead; that was a fact. He prayed to God that at the very least the boy's murderer would sleep less well of nights, although his common sense told him that it was a soft bed that brought sleep to some, no matter the mind's preoccupations.

In the background of his thoughts, Big Tod's bass rolled on. It was good enough, Will decided. A strong Aeneas might carry the play.

" 'Tis enough for now, I pray," Little Tod said, casting the gown aside and reaching for his breeches. "I have the lines by heart; I need not say them more."

"Should you not," Will replied in a better mood, "Aeneas will whisper them sweetly in your ears so that not even the groundlings will hear."

Big Tod laughed genially, not one to remember an offense for more than five minutes. He said, "What may we tonight expect as a reward for our efforts?"

"More than we deserve," Will responded dryly. "Some silver and meat and drink for a moderate man, a piece of good cheese and brown bread. If there's a goose or ham in the bargain we'll give God thanks."

The brothers moved off toward the bar to ease their throats with a drink before the host returned to demand payment. Samuel Peacham, dressed as a man again, drew near to the chief player and took a stool opposite him. Samuel poured a mugful of dark ale, savoring it at his lips before drinking the mug dry. "What shall we do, Will, when the play's done in Chelmsford?"

"London," he replied simply. Behind him Will could hear the brothers whispering at the bar: He nursed his ale; he drank heavily only when he was happy.

Samuel said, "About the lad . . ."

"Aye?"

"I saw you and the constable talking. I know he was asking you about the murder. 'Tis a constable's business. Has he uncovered aught?"

"Nay. He seems as ignorant as we."

"But are we so?"

The question made Will look up. Samuel's narrow crooked face betrayed nothing of his meaning. Will said, "The constable asked me questions; I gave what answers I had."

Samuel sighed heavily, his eyes downcast. " 'Tis the devil's work this, and him the devil's disciple that done it. 'Twas like the butchering of a beast."

" 'Twas the devil's business all right. And yet not Old Nick's, now that I think upon it. There was mortal muscle wielding the knife that killed Richard. Would to God we knew whose."

"If I knew," Samuel said bitterly, "I'd give him what he gave the boy. I'd plumb his guts, pull his boots up through his neck, and make him a long time dying in the bargain."

Will looked into the other player's dark eyes, surprised by this outburst of violent language. Then as suddenly, he caught the man's drift. Samuel feared the blame might be placed upon him. Why, Will was unsure. He said, "I told him that we were all fast friends and no quarrelers among us. So 'tis, is it not?"

"Aye," Samuel replied, a look of relief passing over his face. "And I trust you know that's so for my part."

"I do," Will said reassuringly.

"Townsfolk would be glad to lay the blame for the boy's murder on one of us rather than upon their own were there no more than a jot of proof."

"Indeed so, for they would rather have us entertain them at the end of a rope than upon the stage."

"Well, then," said Samuel confidently, as though he had just clinched an argument in his favor, "you see then how I might be suspected, having just taken over the boy's part and in a fair way of success in it."

Will Shipman looked at Samuel's crooked face and weak chin. "You need not worry about that, I think," he said flatly. "The constable lays the blame on none of us, seems in fact ready enough to accept our words. He may not be witty, but he seems honest. We shall probably have no more trouble of him."

"By the way," Samuel said, anxious now to change the subject, "did you know that the boy spent the last few nights of his life away from the stable?"

Will looked up with surprise. "I did not," he said. "When I sleep, I sleep soundly."

" 'Tis true," Samuel said. "Sometimes I wake at night and walk into the air. Once or twice I have found his place cold in the straw. By signs, he had not slept there at all. And once I heard him come creeping back into the stable just before daybreak. I could hear him coughing and muttering beneath his breath."

"What made you of that?" Will asked, growing interested.

"I made nothing of it, although it does mean that someone was in his mind besides us."

"The girl at the inn, think you?"

"Maybe. But I think not. If I read her face aright, he never quenched her fire; and 'twas the destruction of the poor thing, for sure she took her own life from the want of love."

"Some girl in town then," Will suggested.

"Or at the Hall." Samuel's lips pursed in a smile peculiar to him, his head tilted at a comical angle. Usually Will scorned Samuel's love of gossip, but given the present matter he was prepared to give his full attention.

Will said, "That would have been dangerously done, for great folks care little enough for actors; but when they worm their ways into serving girls' beds, a man's likely to feel a lord's whip upon his back.''

Samuel hesitated; his face broke into a grin. ''Young men are often about such risks for a sweet pair of lips.''

Will shook his head doubtfully.

The men stood and walked to the door and into the inn-yard. ''If it was the girl, or a girl,'' Samuel said, ''the murderer might have been her husband or lover that caught the two in the act. 'Tis a common enough reason for murder.''

''In which case,'' Will reasoned, ''you would think the deed done on the spot. We found the boy's body in the stable. He could not have died there; there would have been an intolerable amount of screaming that would have awakened us all.''

''Unless the screams were muffled. A murderer knows how to keep his business quiet.''

''Yet there was no sign of a struggle. Anyway,'' Will concluded, ''murder done in anger is quickly done. An outraged husband would have stuck him 'neath the ribs and let the devil take the hindmost. Richard's murder was planned—and by someone who had borne a grudge for some time.''

''Well,'' Samuel Peacham replied, not willing to give over his theory, ''it might still have been a husband, one who had uncovered his wife's adultery and wore heavily his horns.''

A light rain began to fall, and Will cursed beneath his breath. Their gear having been carted to the Hall earlier, there was no more to do now but get themselves there. The play, Will decided, was as good as it was going to be.

6

M_{ATTHEW} had told Philip to hitch Pol to the cart and bring both around front of the shop, and it was not long before he heard the mare's two silver bells ringing merrily outside the door. He had already provided himself with a lantern, for they would not make the Hall before nightfall; and the London coach, rumbling toward Chelmsford, was notorious for its disregard of the safety of wayfarers.

Joan lingered at her glass; he occupied himself straightening wares in his shop disarrayed from the day's brisk business. Fidgeting with his new coat, he regretted his constableship, which he had never till this moment felt so burdensome. How he longed to stay by his own fire.

Joan finally appeared at the head of the stairs wearing a French hood with her plain blue gown, and new shoes that showed her tiny feet to advantage. Her brown arms were bare to the elbow, and her round dark features and bright eyes, accustomed as he was to them, struck him as particularly winsome.

He said, "You look beautiful."

"And you, my husband and flatterer, look prosperous and well fed," she responded cheerily, descending the stairs with confidence.

"Best wear a cloak," he warned. "The night will turn chill."

But Alice was already on her way down the stairs with her mistress's cloak beneath her arms. Joan took the cloak with thanks and swung it over her shoulders.

"It does seem a shame to cover such a gown," he said, "with a cloak so worn."

"It fits still, thank God, and shows no bare threads. I'll not be spendthrift and buy another till this one's had its day."

He nodded approvingly, and with a smile that complimented more than her thrift.

The air was indeed chill, and the street darkening. From within windows on the street, flickering candlelight announced the homing of householders, while the air was already heavy with the smoke of cooking fires. After helping Joan to her seat in the cart, Matthew struck his whip lightly on the mare's back; the cart jolted ahead, clattering down the cobblestones at a faster pace than either he or the mare were wont.

On the highroad, Matthew slowed Pol to a more deliberate pace, keeping the cart well to the side of the road, even though there was no more traffic now than an occasional shepherd leading a flock homeward later than usual. In the distance the flat landscape was fast disappearing into darkness. Shadowy trees and hedges now and then broke the thin line of remaining light. There was no wind, but the moon had yet to rise, and Matthew was glad of his lamp.

"Are you hungry," she asked, breaking their silence at last.

"Enough," he responded.

"And comfortable?"

"Here, in the cart?" He shifted uneasily on the wooden seat.

"No, goose, about our going to the Hall." She laughed nervously and poked her husband gently in the ribs. He knew her ways, had recognized where her questions led, but he was content to let her draw him out slowly, teasingly.

57

" 'Tis what you've been waiting for, is it not—what comes of success in trade, a mingling with a better sort of folk?"

"Aye," she replied thoughtfully. "And yet had I thought the entertainment might make you restless beyond enduring, I would have rested content by our own fire."

He said simply, "I must go. Since I am constable, there's no help for it."

"You think still of the murder?"

"That I do. My charge weighs heavily upon me. As yet I have uncovered little more than my own ignorance of how to proceed in such a business."

"Sir Henry has not shown his displeasure?"

"No, and yet he could hardly find satisfaction at the little intelligence I have given him. The lad is dead a full day and his murderer walks as free as we."

She laughed. "La, I have heard that some murders go undiscovered for months, nay years. You are too impatient with yourself. 'Tis very like you. And yet God forbid that any murderer should walk free of an ill conscience."

"A sound conscience would have prevented the act. What it could not hinder it will not mourn. If the murderer walks at all, he walks as free as the wind, and I am now in no place to tell him nay."

"Tomorrow, maybe."

"Aye, tomorrow. The girl at the inn might have told me something had she not taken her own life."

"Then you think she was a part of it all?"

"No doubt."

"But not that she murdered the boy herself and then drowned herself for grief? I shudder to think that any woman would have taken her lover's life so cruelly. For jealousy, think you?"

He laughed, almost to himself, but she heard it above the rumble of the car.

"So," she said in a new but still amiable tone, "this makes you laugh. Do you think I hold my own sex too high?"

"Nay, too lowly," he said, grinning in the darkness. "Such as have power to do great good must have like power to do the devil's work. You do dishonor your sex by supposing women out of the way of murder.''

"Now you do speak as one in the schools, more industrious to trap me than lead me to truth."

They rode along in silence. Then Joan spoke again. "Which—Sir Henry or his lady—played patron to the company?"

"Why do you ask that?" Matthew Stock responded with surprise.

"But to understand," she said. "Chelmsford is out of the way of most players. I know the company has come here at the invitation of Sir Henry, but I know not which of the two had taken the greater interest. It might matter, you know. Sir Henry seems such a solemn gentleman with his broad front. I should not be surprised if his young wife were not the more fond of plays."

"Aye, women like them," he said, baiting her.

She replied earnestly, ignoring his teasing, "Aye, they do, but that is because they like to imagine themselves in other places and conditions."

"I think a man might have such wishes, yet not care for plays."

"Indeed," she said. "And what wishes have you?"

Sensing no danger in the question, he replied boldly, "I feel so out of place at Sir Henry's table that I should wish myself by my own hearth. I am a clothier, no courtier."

"Your father and mother were honest, and you have a place in the town. You need not wipe Sir Henry's boots."

"Granted," he replied. "Yet I am at home in my shop, amongst my men and serving maids. The Hall's a different world, as remote as America from what I know. But still," he added, wishing now to change the subject, "why your interest in the Saltmarshes and their patronage of the players?"

"Because," she replied bluntly, "I wonder if Lady Saltmarsh might have stood more than patron to the boy."

He did not at first understand. She repeated, and he turned abruptly to her as though she had said something unseemly.

"What possesses you to think thusly? Lady Saltmarsh is

59

a fine lady. And though such may be given to wander in their affections, I know nought of her that would suggest she is unfaithful to her husband—and the boy only fourteen.''

"Stranger things have passed betwixt a woman and a boy.''

"Aye, and so they may,'' he said seriously. "And strange beasts I have been told haunt the southern seas but I think not to find them in my tub. Your gossips have been providing you with intelligence across the yard.''

"I bear no tales,'' she said, offended now by his manner. "Although of such you accuse me oft. It is more of what I sense. The knight's lady is indeed beautiful, with a wealth of gowns and lips that might tempt one higher than her husband to crawl beneath her sheets. Yet I have seen her looks to him and his to hers, and I tell you that there is no love lost betwixt 'em.''

"Well,'' he said, "it does not follow that she has played her husband false.''

"It does not,'' she agreed. "And I say not that. What I say, rather, is that she has given her husband cause to suspect her attentions to Richard Mull when she makes the despising of her husband plain to all with eyes.''

" 'Tis not so plain to me,'' he grumbled. But she had given him much to think on, more than set well with him at the moment. Their conversation lapsed into silence. They did not speak again until the lights of the Hall appeared before them like a cluster of little stars low on the horizon.

An old servingman dressed in blue livery led them from the entry into the great chamber, its table spread elegantly with white damask cloth and silver cutlery. A fire blazed at one end of the room; at the other a wooden stage had been constructed for the players. The knight and his lady, dressed very finely, were conversing with a man and woman Matthew recognized as a local squire and his wife. When Lady Saltmarsh approached him, he saw from the corner of his eye Joan suppress a curtsy and gasp of admiration. Cecilia Saltmarsh extended a very white hand and held his longer than he should have supposed. Why, she's not more than a girl herself, he thought.

The Stocks were not seated together at supper, unnatural to them both but, as they supposed, the custom among gentlefolk. From time to time between the courses—there were several sorts of fowl, a large pudding, and a young pig—he glanced sideways at his wife. He was surprised to see her pleasantly engaged with the squire, a tidy little man of about Matthew's own height with ruddy cheeks and tiny eyes. Matthew ate sparingly, his appetite quite gone. When Lady Saltmarsh inquired into his health, he blurted out that it was no worse than it should be, given his age and condition; and he had no sooner done so but felt like the worst fool in the kingdom. This was indeed no place for him.

She had never seen such a table, and for the first few moments in the great dining hall she could do nothing but gawk like a girl just up from the country. A king's table, she thought, and she looked about for what must be her own place, but saw only the ten settings and no smaller convenience in the corner. Her hands were sweaty and before she took those of Cecilia Saltmarsh she pressed her own against her gown.

Cecilia Saltmarsh was indeed a beautiful woman. Joan's practiced eye judged the cost of her ladyship's gown and marveled. Then she was ushered to the heavily laden table. When she was introduced to the squire and his wife, she could only nod stupidly. She was painfully aware of the coarseness of her hands and the plainness of her gown.

At table she had been placed next to the squire and opposite a darkly handsome man introduced to her only as Master Hayforth. Dressed after the French fashion, he kept his eyes on his plate, looking up but once, Joan observed, to answer a question of his host's. She did not recognize his accent, and suspected him of being a Papist, since she had heard that to such the Saltmarshes were sympathetic. Besides, she had detected in his tone a certain clerical whine.

The squire, on the other hand, proved a jolly sort. She allowed him to talk, grateful that his garrulity permitted her shyness to go unobserved. Her pudding done and the last bit of duck cleaned from her plate, she sat back to let her supper settle and herself to take full view of the stage where the players, having suddenly appeared from some recess of the great house, were beginning to gather.

" 'Tis my wife who loves plays," Sir Henry was saying in a loud voice. "And what do you think of them, Mistress Stock?"

The question took her by surprise, for until that moment the knight had seemed not to notice her at all. "In faith," she said haltingly after pausing to collect her thoughts, "I have not seen many, but I would gladly learn wherein their particular virtues lie."

Saltmarsh responded pleasantly, "Then let us hope that this night's entertainment is as edifying as it is delightful."

"Be it not so," Cecilia Saltmarsh added, " 'twil not be the fault of Master Shipman, for I have his word that his company has practiced much and that they be more likely to forget their names than their lines.'

The table responded with polite laughter, and Joan looked into her lap to notice how her fingers had interlocked, as though she were at prayer. Then Cecilia Saltmarsh rose and there was a great shuffling of chairs as the guests positioned themselves to see the stage.

Joan watched admiringly as the young woman walked confidently across the stone floor, noticing the luster of her hair and the shapely curve of her back. When she had returned, the players followed. At their head was he whom Joan took to be their chief, a tall, robust man of about thirty years with full beard and ruddy cheeks. After him came brothers by their looks, and then a small wiry man with black hair, fiery eyes, and hands, she could see at this distance, of a woman's softness. The servingman entered to remove the candles from the table. Sir Henry and his lady turned in their chairs to face the platform; they whispered to one another as conversation at the table subsided and the chief actor mounted to the stage.

These, then, were the old heathen gods. That he could tell even though Will Shipman wore a fine velvet suit not much different from Matthew's own beneath Jupiter's regal purple. The player was seated upon a throne of painted gold, looking every bit the gentleman up from London with silver ringing in his pocket and his beard freshly barbered and perfumed. On his knee dangled his cupbearer and play-fellow, Ganymede. Ganymede was no youth at all but nearer to thirty, his beard discernible beneath the layers of white powder.

Then Jupiter spoke in a rumbling voice of godly author-ity so that for the moment Matthew forgot Will Shipman and really believed himself privy to the Olympians and their disputes. The King of Gods called the boy to him, declaring his love for him, despite Juno. When the boy replied, Matthew realized that Juno was wife to Jupiter and a shrew who, not brooking Jupiter's dalliance, beat the lad soundly. Jupiter flew to the boy's defense, rolling into an impassioned speech of which Matthew could but grasp the gist, and then he gave Ganymede jewels that had belonged to his wife.

Another player, dressed as a great lady, mounted the platform. She berated Jupiter for toying with the boy, ac-cused him of ignoring the hero Aeneas while Juno sub-jected the hero to the peril of sea storms. All this was done in a grand manner, in verse, he reckoned, which was al-together unlike the speech of common folk, being more musical and eloquent, like that of the street vendors who cried out their wares on market day.

Matthew wondered that a god should fondle so insolent a lad, or tolerate such shrewishness from the lady—Venus, he understood, though Jupiter's daughter nonetheless. She strode across the stage and lifted a sinewy arm in expansive gestures, first to the right and then to the left, as she limned her son's perils in a mellow treble neither masculine nor feminine but strangely in between that made Matthew squirm uneasily in his chair. Beneath the layers of white powder, Matthew could trace the lineaments of a man's face, broken teeth, skin marred with the pox, and a nose somewhat east of the perpendicular.

Then Jupiter calmed Venus's rage with a prophecy: All would be turned to the hero's good, though he must first endure hardship and war. The Queen of Love responded, cynically mistrustful of her father's prophecy. Matthew thought of his daughter Elizabeth, how for her her father's word was better than the Queen's Warrant. Then Jupiter sent the other player, who was Hermes, the Messenger of the Gods (so much he had understood from what was said), from the platform to order Neptune to abate his wrath that the hero Aeneas might live, and both he and Ganymede retired from the stage, leaving Venus alone.

Of her speech the constable made little sense, adorned as it was beyond the measure of common tongue. She seemed to speak of her son again, to pronounce a blessing upon him; her voice became softer, as a mother's should, he thought. And she had not finished her part, gesturing still, before two players returned to the platform.

It was Will Shipman again and Samuel Peacham, the latter with the white powder cleared from his skin. Both were garbed as soldiers, the chief actor dressed in a captain's uniform with sword and buckler. This, Matthew guessed, was Aeneas and his companion. Neither man wore a hat, suggesting, he supposed, their recent struggle against the sea.

Except for Jupiter's throne, which had been by this time removed, the platform was quite as bare as before. Aeneas extended a brawny arm to the wall of the chamber, identifying it as the wall of Carthage; Venus crouched at the corner of the platform as though behind a bush. Now Aeneas strolled proudly around the stage as became a hero while the two companions related the woe of their travels. When Venus discovered herself (Matthew marveled that she could not be seen crouched there so plainly), Aeneas did not recognize his mother, but introduced himself to her, boasting of his courage. When she departed the platform, Aeneas realized that it was Venus to whom he had spoken. Then the actors left the stage and the servingman entered to light the candles at the great table.

"How did you like the first act, Master Constable?"

Matthew, as though awakened from a dream, responded slowly to Sir Henry's question.

"I think it not like anything I have seen, sir. The actors

play their parts admirably, ne'er missing a line as I could tell. Their speech is marvelously fashioned, quite poetic I would say,"

He paused with embarrassment, wondering that he should have said so much, but Saltmarsh did not seem annoyed at his answer. The knight smiled pleasantly and sipped wine from his goblet. In a moment his attention was fixed upon another guest.

"I think Master Peacham a most engaging Dido," Cecilia Saltmarsh was saying. "He that would play that unfortunate queen must know how to weep as a woman as well as sue for a gentleman's favors."

"You should play such a part, my dear," Saltmarsh said, bowing gracefully in his wife's direction.

"I might, were it seemly that ladies so display themselves. But, as in all things else, plays are men's work, though they be to a woman's pleasure."

Her remark was met with laughter around the table, as though it concealed some wit. Matthew looked to Joan and found her eyes meeting his. At the moment the squire was addressing some remark to her right ear. Then he saw her smile and look down at her hands on the table. Matthew thought of the play he had just witnessed and of the lad Ganymede perched so securely on Jupiter's knee. He had heard of such loves between man and boy, but such was beyond his fathoming. He found it difficult to think about.

She sat transfixed, so intent that only a vigorous shaking of her shoulders would have drawn her eyes from the stage, the players, the magnificent scene. When the play was done and the candles relighted, it was as though she must swim up to the surface of her life after having held her breath for an hour or more in this place, both the great room of the Hall and somewhere else all together. It was all, Joan reflected, so pathetical—Aeneas's misfortunes, his moving account of the great city's fall. Dido's hopeless love on the altar of her beloved's duty. She might have wept for it had she not been in company. What had impressed her most had been Queen Dido herself, tall and stately with features most perfectly white and rouged so that her cheeks seemed aflame with life and gowned and slippered in the old-fashioned elegance of an embroidered chemise of fine Raynes linen partly hidden by a crimson cloak. She had almost forgotten that this graceful feminine figure was a man—and yet not so, for from time to time his falsetto would break, allowing his tone to fall to a more masculine depth that betrayed the player's mature years.

So this was a play, she marveled.

Varnell had seen better, and the thought of it gave him no little satisfaction under present circumstances, seated as he was obscurely at the table's end. At least, he reflected bitterly, he had been allowed to sit with the guests and not shuttled off to the kitchen to feed with the servants. And now in return for a middling supper he must endure this evocation of musty tomes whose moldy tales he had so hated at school and for which none but melancholic wenches and pedantic schoolmasters cared but a groat. The players marched the stage like laborers seeking their tools, delivered their lines as though they understood but half, fitted their mouse-eaten robes most ridiculously, and mumbled in their beards by turns. He that played Dido so scurvily was the worst, whining out his lines like a cat in the bag, pleading with his mistress to drown him not, for he was a good cat, as many a mouse caught in the buttery might affirm. Besides, he had drunk with the man within the week. Varnell knew him to be a fool and cutpurse.

Disgruntled absolutely, he turned his attention from the stage to the table. His employer's back was between him and the players, looming like a shadow in the half-darkness, well fed, well satisfied, and powerful. To his right, his mistress leaned upon one slender arm. Toward her husband, he noted. He thought, She hates him more than I, and doubtless for similar reasons. On both sides of the table sat those who were no better than he and yet more honored here. There was the priest, morose, secretive, looking as though he had his salvation by patent and waited nothing but to be lifted up to his glorification. Others, besides the cloddish constable and his wife, were the small fry of the town. All sat like blocks, or like children watching the devil dance in a bright fire. What could they know, who could not find this piece as wretchedly done as conceived, Kit Marlowe's reputation notwithstanding. Not one month past he had seen Ben Jonson's *Poetaster* upon the Blackfriars stage. Now there was a play with meat. He wondered that his employer should bid to his table such as these, whom fortune had declared must serve and not be served. He had detected Sir Henry's oily condescension to the rout at entrance. What game was he playing now? Or his lady, who on this occasion played so sweetly his accomplice?

Varnell looked up from his musings to see the dark eyes of the priest fixed upon him, and he shuddered.

The play done, Saltmarsh and his lady rose from the table. The players were sent to the buttery, where, Saltmarsh assured them, they might have a free hand to fill their own stomachs and quench their thirst, but not before they had been roundly applauded for their efforts. Then the guests bid their hosts farewell with many thanks.

"A word with you, Master Constable, before you go," Saltmarsh said as Matthew and Joan were about to follow the servingman to the door.

Matthew paused while his wife went on ahead with the other guests. "I thank you, sir, once again, both for such meat and for the play, of which I had never before seen the like."

Saltmarsh responded in what was almost a whisper, "You see, then, Master Stock, what table we keep here and what cheer. These are persons who 'twould be to your good to know, since they may help you in a business way. But pray oblige me in this: do not lessen your efforts to resolve me in the players' boy's death, for I have this night by Master Hayforth just come from Southend that word of the murder has spread the county and 'twere unseemly if in my first year of my magistracy I did not bring the murderer to speedy justice. You know my mind, then?"

"Aye, sir, and do promise you once again. It is only that in this case there are so few clues."

Saltmarsh smiled grimly. "Perhaps, but there is one who knows everything in the matter, and it is your commission to find him out and quickly. My wife and I expect to depart for London later in the week.''

"You may in all things trust me to do my duty," Matthew said earnestly.

Saltmarsh patted him on the arm. "I do, I do," he said, "and now I must look to the players, who will have their reward, I hope, not too rowdily."

Joan waited him on the steps. A groom had brought around the cart, which now stood ready at hand in the drive. Matthew helped his wife in and then himself, and both rode silently until they had come to the gate and passed beneath its imposing height.

"That was a night we shall not soon forget," he said.

"I think not," she replied.

"How liked you the play?"

"It was strangely pleasing. Such fine speeches, although I near wept at Dido's end, poor lady, of such quality and then to be deserted by her lover."

He smiled in the darkness to himself. "But would a woman so love a man to cast herself into the flames for him?''

"Men have done so for the truth of their religion," she returned.

"Yes, but hardly unless pressed to it."

Joan reasoned, "Perhaps she was. The heart may be as compulsive as a wicked queen to drive men and women to madness and beyond."

He retorted, "I think such be the devil's work. God has made us free to choose the evil from the good, and to believe or not without constraint. If a broken heart has the strength to drive one to self-slaughter, 'tis no better than a prince puffed up in his pride and deserves no pity."

She considered this. Then she said, "I see my husband is a moralist as well as constable. I know not where his competence shall have an end."

He chuckled and threw one arm around her shoulder, for the night was cold. "I fear I am competent only as thy husband, Joan, and then only in part, but as a theologian or moralist I am none, only that I try to give heed to good short sermons and read the scripture of a Sunday. As for my constableship, I fear I am in danger of losing that."

"Is it that of which Sir Henry spoke as we were leaving?"

"Aye, it quite took from me the joy of supper to think that I have made so little headway against my own ignorance. 'Tis a point of honor with him to have the murder solved and quickly. He intends to leave the Hall at week's end for London."

"Surely he would not be adverse to allowing more time, should it be needed. The boy's death is hardly cut and dried. There were no witnesses."

"He regards not that and reminds me still of my commission."

"Are you sorry now that you accepted the office?"

He thought before replying. "Indeed I am; but having it, I must serve dutifully, no matter the outcome. Tomorrow I will go again to speak with the players. I suspect that they know more of Richard Mull's private matters than they are willing to admit. Such folk keep close counsel. And I think they at the Hall are also involved, though I cannot say how."

"Then you do think my suspicion of Cecilia Saltmarsh be more than idle gossip?"

"At table they seemed happily coupled. She is a beautiful lady, hardly more than twenty, I should think. I cannot fathom why such should not get along, since her husband is a proper enough man and, although twice her age, evidently not unkind. I cannot therefore think that she would have cause to chase a mere boy who brought nothing to her but . . ."

He paused searching for the word, which she supplied: "A young body?"

"Shame, woman," he retorted with mock severity. "Your mind doth too much run in such ways. Soon I will be thinking myself too old for such a one as you."

"We are of near the same years, Matthew. And of love you have always been my only teacher. If I now grow ripe as a student, 'tis yourself who art much to blame."

He said, "Tush, I have gone to school to you, Joan, as

you well know. No, that some strange lust has perverted her ladyship's way I hope to doubt. What I think rather is that the boy may have made some suit to her, which her refusing drove him into a passion or perhaps into a quarrel with one of his fellows.''

"You love the plain road, husband, and could not see perversion were it hanging on our strong oak like a child's bauble. Did it not the more make you fit for my husband, I would lament that your very innocence should so undermine your ability as constable.''

He laughed heartily. "Innocent? I?''

"Innocent, you,'' she replied quickly. "He that can think so little evil will never find the rat in the cellar, he himself too honest to sneak or steal.''

"I have never thought of myself as such, but as a plain man, no better or worse than my fellows.''

" 'Tis not virtue I am accusing you of but innocence. They be different.''

He laughed again. "And now who plays the moralist?''

He felt the touch of her cold lips upon his cheek and drew her close to him.

"Full stomachs and wine have made us both merry,'' she said and, looking up, realized that they were already on High Street and not a minute from their own door.

He drew the cart to a halt, dismounted, went up to the door and began knocking vigorously.

"Pray God on such a cold night our man is not himself fast asleep. We must freeze here if we wait until morning.''

His blows rattled the windowpane. From the rear of the house the hounds Molly and Col yelped peevishly.

"The neighborhood will wake,'' she warned from the cart.

"I do fear it,'' he replied, knocking again impatiently.

A light appeared at the window, and soon husband and wife could hear Philip unbarring the door and mumbling prayers under his breath. "I heard your first knock,'' the old man growled, half in apology, half in protest, "but thought it was a dream and rolled over in my bed.''

"Well,'' Matthew said sternly, "let us in now or we'll die of the cold.''

Joan helped herself down from the cart and led her husband through the door.

"Mind that the house is fast again, and do quiet the hounds. We've wakened them with our beatings," he said. He led the way with lantern to their chamber above, where he quickly built a fire.

They warmed themselves without speaking and then she sighed and said, "I am for bed."

"And I with you," he replied.

Under the heavy quilt he drew near her just before sleep, letting his hand find its way under her night garment to the small of her back, warm and soft as it had been the twenty years he had known her as husband. He fell asleep and dreamed of the walls of Carthage, and of Aeneas, and of the boy Ganymede whom Jupiter loved.

7

THE CHAMBER that Hayforth had been given was cramped, and the servant had brought no wood for the fire. He shivered, reluctant to undress, listening instead for the soft sound of footfalls beyond his door.

It had been a long day, most of which he had spent on horseback. His muscles were sore; his head ached with drink. His host had proved polite but suspicious. Such, the priest guessed, was the man's nature. Cecilia Saltmarsh had prevailed upon him to stay the night and perhaps another until he should be sufficiently rested to continue his journey to London. She said she desired his counsel, and that he might say mass in the chapel, although to do so might be risky. All of that had been predictable enough, but not his recognition of Samuel Peacham in Marlowe's play. Neither the intervening years since their last meeting nor the heavy makeup on Peacham's face could erase the memory of those oddly twisted features, the small frightened but intent eyes, the chin that seemed to disappear into the hollow of the thin neck.

The priest had shared a room with Peacham and Marlowe ten years before when the three were postulants at the Catholic college at Rheims, and earlier Hayforth and Marlowe had been fellow students at Cambridge. At Rheims they had in fact been spies, eager for news of Papist plots on the continent and names of Papist sympathizers and agents in England. Peacham and Marlowe had given over such services, Peacham becoming an actor in an obscure company, Marlowe going on to make a name for himself as a playwright. Only the priest retained his old profession as a spy, his present business being the discovery and undermining of fresh conspiracies on his native soil. A friend had written Hayforth of Marlowe's death. How like Marlowe to end that way—at a reunion of confederates at Eleanor Bull's tavern at Deptford. Ingram Frizer, Robert Poley, Nicholas Skeres—Hayforth had known them all, and a fine lot of devils they were. Now Marlowe was dead, murdered in a quarrel over the reckoning. Well, what of that? Walsingham, their old employer, was as cold. They might both rot, for all Hayforth cared now. But how clearly his mind's eye recalled the young playwright's face. In the stillness of the chamber he could almost hear yet the golden tongue of him whose young piety had withered in the fire of the intellect and whose infinite aspiration had been tempered only by sudden fits of cynicism and melancholy.

They had shared rooms above a carpenter's shop in the French city, descanting on the absurdities of French manners, their poor allowance from Walsingham, and the ridiculousness of Papistry while they had hatched plots against fellow students and pooled intelligence that might be sent home through the network of Walsingham's spies. It was a dirty life that might have shamed him in the recalling of it had custom not long ago taken the vice from it. Now, near forty, he was too old to begin another profession (if profession spying could be called). He was too proud to play courtier, too cynical for churchman, too lazy for the law, too practiced a dissembler for honest service at home. Such was the fate of a spy—to become so proficient in the devious art that even one's mother must hide the key to the breadbox. Besides, he now had the office of priest down pat; he could pray, hear confessions, celebrate mass, preach sugary sermons, squirm and grovel before the well-to-do like any priest in hell. He could tell lies to shame the devil, knew more tricks of policy than a cardinal and more ways to slander, maim, and poison than the Pope himself.

The play had brought it all back with startling clarity. Indeed, Marlowe had written *Dido* in the next chamber at Cambridge, between translations of Seneca and snatches of Machiavelli, whom Marlowe had studied as though they were holy writ. Even as the players had spoken their lines, the priest recalled their author's voice through the thin walls reciting the work to himself until all the syllables were numbered and marshaled into rattling rows and made fit for such persons as should speak them. But the priest's nostalgia was now poisoned by a fear that Peacham should have recognized him at table and, remembering their earlier association as agents, conclude logically that he remained in the business and, purposely or inadvertently, let the fact slip, to Saltmarsh.

The knight he knew to be the sort of Catholic who would have welcomed the return of the old religion but who would do little to further it. His devotion was at best lukewarm, as far as the priest could tell. Cecilia Saltmarsh, on the other hand, seemed genuinely pious, or so he had inferred from several private conferences he had had with the lady at Rheims and from her invitation to visit her and her husband at Chelmsford upon his return to England. His acceptance of the invitation had been encouraged by his superiors in the government who were anxious to identify any member of the gentry willing to hear mass in chapel or play host to a disguised priest. He dreaded to think of Saltmarsh's response to the information that he had given bed and board to one who might be his undoing.

He had found the guests of the evening mildly interesting despite his weariness from travel, but perhaps only because they were different from the lot he was used to. Except for Saltmarsh's secretary. The priest knew his kind. The constable and his wife he found quite droll, both plump and dark like gypsies. Then there was the garrulous squire who went on about the price of wool as though it were the man's own skin that was to be shorn and his thin-as-a-bean wife who ate as solemnly as a Puritan at meeting. The pompous scrivener had pronounced upon stage plays, the quality of the pudding, the merits of city versus country life, new cures for mad dogs, and ways to build a mousetrap to catch three of the vermin at a swipe. It was all like the comedy of the old style. And, finally, Peacham as Queen of Carthage. What irony had been there. Yes, he had been queen all right, as any of the Cambridge gallants who had had him as bedfellow might testify were they willing to make their curious tastes known.

The play done, the priest had walked toward the door with Cecilia Saltmarsh at the same time her husband had separated himself from the others to say some words in private to the constable. She had asked for an interview in private late that evening when the guests were gone and her husband had gone to carouse with the players.

He heard no knock at his door; she entered suddenly with a finger at her lips commanding him to silence. She was dressed in a thin loosely fitted chemise over which she had thrown a finely woven shawl. He noticed that her feet were bare and small, almost like a child's. She did not wait for him to speak but took the chair.

"The hour is not too late for this?" she asked.

"Needs of the soul must be met as they occur." He fell easily into his old role. He knew the voice, the gestures, just how the lips were pursed and the hands folded prayerfully as though the interlocking fingers alone might draw deity into the room.

"I am obliged to you, sir, for allowing me to come hither so late for spiritual comfort. I ask you to be discreet, however, for I would not have my devotions the talk of servants." She paused to allow the significance of her remark to settle.

He said, "Perhaps, then, we should delay our talk until tomorrow?"

"No . . . the house then will be in confusion and the servants occupied with packing. Sir Henry and I go to London later in the week."

"How may I serve you, lady?"

"By listening," she replied softly. "I am a most unhappy woman."

In the half darkness of the chamber her face was white, her hair loose about her shoulders. She is prepared for bed, he thought, yet she comes here boldly. Had she remembered their appointment at the last minute or come so by design? The priest was no novice in the devices of women, but he was prudent enough to allow her to show her hand before he would wager his own. Women, he knew from the varieties of his experiences, could be more subtle than men in such matters. They could also be naive, and he had often found himself amused at the way women of refined manners could treat a priest as though he were not a man at all but some sexless, passionless thing. Yet he knew enough of the world's ways to proceed with caution. Cecilia Saltmarsh was a beautiful woman, but she was also the wife of a peevish knight who would not hesitate to cut his throat for overstepping bounds.

She asked, "You are pensive?"

"I only wait for you to speak, lady. You say you are an unhappy woman. Certainly with such a husband and house and servants you could not want much?"

"I do not have things I seem to have," she said mournfully as her gaze fell downward to the folds of her lap.

"Things you seem to have," he echoed.

"My husband has no love for me."

"Surely, madam, you are mistaken. He does seem a most affectionate and generous lord."

"So he does seem," she said bitterly. "That's his public manner. In private he is much different, cold, often angry without cause. We do not share the same bed."

He considered his words carefully. " 'Tis not uncommon between husband and wife that quarrels force them apart for a season. They sleep in different chambers until cold sheets and silent walls bring them back to their senses and their mates. Have hope, madam. Despair is 'gainst God's will. You are far too young and, may I say, beautiful to consider yourself forsaken. If your husband has been cruel, indifferent, he may be kind and loving yet if you will be but patient."

"I fear he is beyond the redemption of which you speak. Nightly he carouses, and I know not where. Even now he

76

is below with the players and may drink till dawn. After, he proceeds to other friends.''

"Other friends?"

"I do not know their names. Women of the town perhaps. My husband likes women."

"You are accusing your husband of adultery," he said. "That's a most grievous sin."

"Yet I have no proof, only a feeling."

"If proof might be found, you might do nothing still, yet no wife should suffer her husband's continued infidelity."

She said after a pause. "You are a kind man, even for a priest."

"I serve God in treating humanely his children."

"I wonder," she began, "if I may be so bold as to approach even more private matters?"

"What passes here," he replied, "will not pass beyond these walls, though death threatened. I am under solemn oath."

"Not all priests honor their vows."

" 'Tis true, lady," he admitted, rising from the bed and stepping toward the cold hearth of the chamber. "Priests are but men. They suffer temptations as other men must. Their priesthood should serve as an iron garment through which no carnal lust might pierce, and yet it sometimes does. I have known fallen priests. Perhaps circumstances mount such a battery against their oaths that not even a saint might resist."

"Your pity for your fallen brethren argues you a man of God indeed," she said.

"It argues me a man, no more," he replied simply.

"Are you a man?" she asked.

Her question took him suddenly, and it was spoken to his back so that he could not read in her face the implication of the question. When he turned to her, her head was down, her hands placidly in her lap.

"I am sometimes tempted," he said, returning to the bed.

"To what sort of things, may I ask?" She faced him boldly now. "You can count it but a woman's curiosity.

77

Yet 'tis not an idle one, for I have revealed unto you the cause of my distress and yet you have said nothing of your own.''

"My distress? Why do you suppose I am distressed?"

She stood and walked to where he sat upon the bed, raising a hand to his brow as though she were reading the lines in his forehead. "I can read your sorrow, just here, above the brow . . . in the little furrows."

He admired her wit, seeing now her design, the chain of words by which she hoped to bind him. Now he cared nothing for her husband, for the risk. "I am a priest still," he said, but with enough regret in the tone to render it an invitation for her to proceed further.

"And a man?" she whispered, moving closer to him. "As a man, do you find me comely?"

He hesitated, uncertain now of just the right words. "I think you are the most beautiful woman I have known."

"I am not dressed.," she protested halfheartedly.

"Men were created perfect. They are most so, then, when as God made them."

Her eyes were large; they shone brightly in the candlelight, full of knowledge and with a masculine confidence he found strangely appealing. He could tell that his sophistry pleased her.

"You are eloquent, sir. In what church did you learn so to please a woman's ear?"

"It is you, lady, who makes me eloquent. But I would express myself in more than words."

She made no show to move when he grasped her wrists, but remained erect. Her lips formed a slight smile. She said, "You may express yourself as you see fit. We are quite alone here."

As he reached for her waist, her shawl slipped from her shoulders, leaving them bare and white in the half darkness. He could see her perfectly round breasts beneath the sheer cloth of her chemise as he pulled her toward him.

"You are passionate," she whispered after they had lain together for a while. "Pull the blanket over us, for God's sake."

"You are modest?" he grunted drowsily.

"I am cold," she said. "You make love more like a soldier than a priest."

He could feel her thighs and stomach tremble in the cold beneath him. He said, "I have been both in my time."

She pushed him suddenly from her. His desire spent, he rolled over on his back, staring into the dark of the ceiling. The candle had burned low.

"Should this be known to my husband, sir priest . . ." She did not finish the threat.

Without turning to her again, he said, "Do you do your own murders, my lady?"

She cursed, grabbed her smock, and pulled it over her head. She found her shawl where it had dropped in the rushes and walked quickly to the door. She turned to him as though to speak again, but said nothing. The priest turned his eyes to the wall, cursed the cold, the servant who had brought no wood, and the ill luck that had brought him to this place.

Varnell snuffed out his single candle and crawled sleepily beneath the covers. Voices and music still drifted up from the great hall below, muffled by heavy oak timbers and plaster and merging with the first shapes of sleep. He dreamed he was back in Cambridge in his old chamber before a pile of books and scattered papers. From the corner of his eye he could see a great brown rat munching upon one of the books. The sight disgusted him, and he drew closer to the book and saw that it was the Bishops' Bible in heavy black print and a rich leather cover. The rat ate and ate until the book's cover was completely consumed, and then it began to feed on the text itself. Varnell tried vainly to push the rat away, but the creature ignored him, twitched its whiskers, and continued to eat. He could not make his arms move; they felt pinned to his sides. The rat seemed to grow larger as it ate, larger and larger until it began to fill the chamber, crowding the secretary into one corner, its foul odor making his gorge rise. Weeping with frustration and terror, he awoke, his body drenched with sweat. It was a long while before he could fall asleep again.

Deep in his cups, Saltmarsh leaned heavily upon the table, his arms outstretched. Dark liquor flowed from the corners of his mouth. He thrust out his jaw at the player defiantly. "Say you?" he snarled.

Samuel Peacham, too drunk himself to be fearful or respectful, sneered back. "A woman's part is no meaner than a man's. It takes more part—part—particular wit, and 'tis not easily won, for few there be that has it, damme." He threw his head back with bleary satisfaction.

The knight thundered, "Then I say you have it not, for you played Queen Dido most wretchedly and made me want to laugh when I should have shed more tears for the poor lady then Hecuba for her lost children."

Saltmarsh thrust himself back from the bench with a triumphant grunt. Samuel Peacham had fallen asleep, his head in his plate.

"More wood, Daniel, more wood," Saltmarsh thundered, "or by all that's holy I'll have your arse for fuel."

His livery askew, the old servingman limped into the chamber with his arms full of wood. His sober industriousness put a pall on the festivities that for an hour past had begun to wane from sheer monotony. Big Tod was nowhere to be seen. Will Shipman crouched by the firelight, his shaggy head resting upon his knees, deep in thought or sleep while Little Tod snored peacefully nearby.

Suddenly Will raise his head, looked at his companion, and brought his hand down flat on the player's belly. "Up, Little Tod, the feast grows stale."

Little Tod swallowed a snore and looked around him wildly. Upright but still confused, he said, "Is there trouble?"

"Anon, I think," the chief player replied, his voice low.

The men stumbled to their feet and walked unsteadily toward the table where Saltmarsh and Samuel Peacham had finished their quarrel and collapsed.

Will said, " 'Tis time to bid our host good night and leave, Samuel. We've taken his meat and drink and more than we deserved, though we shall thank him nonetheless and pray he think kindly on us when we next pass this way.''

Samuel did not respond, but moaned softly; Saltmarsh looked up vaguely, his eyes red with drink. Little Tod began to help Samuel Peacham to his feet, and then he and Will helped carry the still unconscious player from the chamber. They stopped at the kitchen, where Big Tod had gone earlier with the Welsh girl.

Will called out at the door. " 'Tis time to bid good night, friend. Say thanks to the wench, for 'twill be some time before we pass this way again.''

From the corner of the kitchen came a rustle of clothing and muffled oaths. Will called out again, this time in a more commanding voice. Then Big Tod responded from the corner, "I come, friends; pray leave me but a moment more, for I would learn this Welsh before I die.''

Will swore under his breath and motioned to Little Tod to move forward. Though he was slight of build, Samuel Peacham was all dead weight; unconscious, he would give them no help, and the men had trouble getting him down the stone steps into the courtyard. There, Will could see Sir Henry's servants had loaded their wagon. He and Little Tod strained to get the unconscious player aboard. Then Little Tod went to the stable for their horse while Will mounted the driver's seat, musing upon the night's business. Within a few minutes Big Tod came bounding down the steps, exuberantly awake and grinning. Will wanted to hear about the girl, but now he was tired and not a little disgusted, although he was not sure about what. Big Tod's story would have to wait until tomorrow. When Little Tod returned with the horse, they hitched it to the wagon in silence. Then Will let out one last mouth-filling oath, and the wagon moved forward while great clouds of night covered and uncovered the moon.

Her hair was auburn, thick like his own, and it framed a delicate face with wide-set eyes, thin nose, small mouth. She spoke softly in a voice thick with her Welsh, but an English nonetheless he would readily hear. That is why when Gwen had asked him if he would help her with the tray of plates he had not hesitated to follow her to the kitchen, the cooks having gone to bed an hour before.

When she invited him to sit with her, Big Tod readily consented, settling with her by the fire.

She said, "You are wondrous strong."

"Aye, it helps if there's man's work to be done."

"Or maid's, 'twould appear," she said with a lilt in her voice.

"My father was a carpenter," he began, "but I could not abide the work. I went to London when I was no more than twelve and found mischief enough."

Gwen poured more of the malmsey for them both and said, "I am from the west country. My mother and father are dead. I've but one sister, married now. We never got along. I'm best here."

"It must be a great thing to serve so grand a lady. Does she treat you well?"

"Aye, she does that, although every now and then she speaks sharply and calls me slut. Yet God knows I'm honest."

He looked at her directly. "You're fair. Does Sir Henry leave you be?"

She looked up at the question, then suppressed a giggle. "He? Well, he might leave a poor girl of his house be when he has such others to do his bidding."

Interested, Big Tod said, "And who might such ladies be? I should think a woman such as his lady would hold any man to continence."

"She's cold to him," the Welsh girl replied, shaking her head.

Big Tod took the measure of Gwen's face and figure. She's young, he thought, twelve or thirteen by the eyes and hands. Her hands were soft and freckled.

"You mean they have little love for each other?"

"Little that I have seen, though his lordship be as amorous as any Frenchman to hear his wife tell of it—yet not with her. That is her complaint, that she is young and fair but neglected and must pine away like a widow with a cold bed and little hope of remarrying."

She was thin, flat-chested like a boy, but her eyes were blue and gleamed in the firelight. Aroused, he shifted himself so that their thighs touched near the hearth. She did not move away.

"And to whom does his lordship take a liking—some lady of the town perhaps?"

"I cannot be sure," she answered. "We have little company here, save for Master Hayforth, who has this evening come from the coast and will be gone hence in a day or two. He is a priest, I think, for both my master and mistress be of the old faith, although neither is eager to own it."

"I marked him for that," Big Tod said knowingly.

She said, "He's no ordinary priest, I can tell you that."

"What do you mean?" he asked, his curiosity aroused.

She bent forward and to the side so their foreheads nearly touched and she whispered, "Not a half hour since I saw my mistress go in her nightgown to his chamber. And to my knowledge she remains there still." She leaned back, her lips curled in satisfaction.

"If he be priest, then maybe she confesses to him as is the custom among Papists."

"In faith, I think she opens more to him than her heart, for I have seen her look at him, and a proper man he is, though a priest. Can you blame her should she want more comfort in her bed than a cold recollection of her wedding night three years before?"

He said, "Then I wish her and her like joy of whatever sheets she may find, for even great ladies must needs be satisfied, as they be no different in that regard than their waiting maids."

She looked up at him sharply, as though to chide his sauciness. Then her face broke into a smile. "You turn insolent."

"I cry you mercy"—he laughed, appreciating her good humor—"for if I have said aught but what is God's truth may I choke upon it."

"Well," she said, pursing her lips thoughtfully. "I cannot deny what I have never known of myself. I am a maid."

"You have no friend here, then?"

"None. Daniel the servingman has an old wife and more children than he can count. There are other servants, but I see them rarely. I would accompany my mistress to church would she go herself, but since she and the master are of the old faith they will not hear a sermon of one of the new churchmen but claim illness or travel if they are brought to account for their absence. And yet I would and would not have a man. The girl at the inn was of my own years. She loved, I have heard, one of your company and she died from the grief of it, so sad was she at his death. Here I might die not of grief but of loneliness and take my maidenhead with me to the grave."

"That would be a great pity," he said, smiling.

"Think you so?" she said.

"My friends drink late," he said. "Let us heap more logs upon the fire. We'll not be bothered here?"

" 'Tis unlikely," she said. When he returned with the wood and the fire was blazing again, she drew close to him.

"I had a sister such as you." He leaned forward and kissed her, pleased to find her lips warm and responsive.

She said, "I will pretend you are a great bear, such as I saw once in London with my mistress. He stood like a man, but when he roared I felt a fear of him in the base of my spine. He was chained and bleeding. I felt pity for him . . . so powerful, and yet to be chained."

"You are a strange one to think on such things now."

"Now?" she said, loosening herself from his embrace and facing him squarely. "I think of you as a great bear because you are marvelously strong and a tall man, without fear, I should think. For all I know, you have killed men in your time."

"Never," he said, laughing, "though I have come close to it."

"See," she said triumphantly. "You are a bear in truth, for bears be fighters by nature, and they give their enemies great hugs until they die."

"You think much of death. Is it the girl of the inn whom you think upon?"

" 'Tis the boy, rather," she said. "For he was wondrous fair of face and parts, almost like a woman, yet he indeed had manly parts about him.''

"And how know you that?" he said to tease her. "Even now you confessed yourself a maid.''

Gwen hesitated, staring into the fire with her back half turned from him. "If you be my friend in truth," she said, "then I shall share a secret with you, but you must promise to tell none other.''

"You have my promise, though they put me upon the rack.''

"Richard Mull was a great favorite of my mistress. Many times I have seen the two in company, and once when I brought my lady fresh linen I found the two together in her bed. She I could not see, save for two bare arms curled about his back and her gold hair trailing upon the pillow as though it were floating on a stream. He was without his shirt, and I blushed to look upon his naked backsides. My lady moaned softly; he lay still as though he were dead—except that once I saw his ankle jerk.''

"If his back was toward you, how knew you that it was Richard Mull and not some other?''

"Because when I entered upon them, I let out a gasp of surprise and he quickly withdrew from her and turned upon his side to look me in the face. In faith, he gave me such a look that I believe had he another weapon about his body than that he had just used he would have been my death.''

For a moment he pondered her story, then he asked, "What did your mistress say, being found so inconveniently?''

"Why not a word. 'Twas as though she had not seen me at all, but lay still moaning softly in her sheets as if she had been given some potion. Would to God I had it, for I would know such pleasure myself.''

" 'Tis passing strange," he said. "And she said nothing to you thereafter?''

"Aye, and more so because as I quickly left the chamber I heard Richard Mull mutter to her that they had been seen by the serving girl. At that I heard my mistress laugh and say that if they had been seen by such as I, I might learn to fall upon my back properly when I came of age.''

"You are a wise one for your years," he said.

"I am not as young as you might think, for I heard my mother say before she died that 'twas not the time but the quality that made one what she was, and in faith I think that's true of my small case. I do not lack the years of knowledge, save, of course, in the matter of my maidenhead, which I have yet to surrender to any man."

"Ah," he said, "that magic draft your lady took when you found her with Richard beneath the sheets. I am not surprised. Richard, unlike some of us, could have any woman, erect or fallen upon her back, in less time than it took a falcon to scoop up a field mouse. But what of her your lady's husband? Though he be as cold as a dead man's hand, I wonder that he should have suffered such doings."

"And you should wonder the more did you know that he indeed knew of their lovemaking. Sir Henry was present at the time."

Big Tod was so astonished at her words that he asked her to repeat them.

"In the very chamber," she said. "There were three of them, the two upon the bed and the master in his chair at the other side of the room."

"And they cared not that he watched them?" he asked incredulously.

"I think not. I could not see his face at his cuckolding but he was there as witness, and I think so prominently that it must have been with his wife's permission."

"Or at his command," Big Tod suggested. " 'Tis wondrous strange this household that you serve."

"Aye," she agreed.

"Sir Henry has said nothing to you about what you saw?"

"He does not speak to me two words from one week to the other on any account. He may not have heard me gasp for breath, or if he did he may have thought it a mouse in the corner not worth regarding at the moment.

"Another man would have slit Richard's throat, his wife's, and yours too to keep his disgrace well within doors," he mused. "I am fond of you, girl. This is no safe house, for where there's such goings-on murderous thoughts find a ready nest. I advise you to seek work else-where."

She turned to him appealingly. "Where should I go, without friends or family?"

"Let me think on it," he said. "I will talk to our chief, Will Shipman."

"You will not betray what I have told you?" she pleaded.

"Nay, I have given my word. I'll not tell your secrets or those of this house, but you must guard this all in your heart, for I would have nothing ill befall you. Be wary of your master and mistress. Tread softly in their presence, and do not go into Sir Henry's alone. I trust not the man, be he magistrate or no."

She looked at him desperately. "Think you my life's in danger?"

"I think," he said slowly, "that Richard Mull has paid the price of his pleasures and should your employers sud-denly take a mind to keep this business to themselves, your death would follow like a lank hound after a bitch in heat. What I will say to Will Shipman—for he's a good man despite some past differences—is that I know a girl such as yourself handy in the mending of garments, man's and woman's."

She interrupted. "If you say so, you will say true, for I have such skill."

"Then you might travel with us. It is not an easy life, yet there are worse. We are sometimes chased from the towns and fall foul of the law or the Puritan folk, but we see much of the country, breathe fresh air, and live by our wits, and there is some joy in that."

"You have given me much to think upon," she said soberly.

"And you me," he replied. "We came here by invita-tion of Sir Henry and his lady, but it may be that God will turn it all to good."

It was at that moment that big Tod heard the familiar voice of Will Shipman in the corridor. "I think the feast be done. You are best for bed."

"Alone with only my maidenhood for company?"

He kissed her full on the mouth. Her lips tasted of sweet malmsey and she kissed soft, not hard like the city girls whose lips were often calloused and full of sores.

"God keep you," she said.

He got to his feet awkwardly, his left leg numb from his having sat upon it for such a length of time. From the outer room he heard once again the call of his fellows, and he returned the call with an oath. He gave her a last kiss and said, "Look to your safety. Best tell no other what you have told me."

She nodded and he joined his comrades, looking back but once to admire her slender silhouette in the firelight.

8

MATTHEW rose early the next morning and dressed as though he knew exactly what he was about. He kissed Joan, stuffed his pockets with cheese and biscuits to eat on the way, then went into the street to find the apprentice boy just finishing his sweeping and the town awakening to another cold gray morning. Greeting a handful of neighbors like him already about their business, he walked past the silversmith's, the greengrocer's, the bondsman's, the scrivener's, and the half dozen apprentices who hung around the bakery to smell bread bake and exchange droll stories on their masters' time. He was near the edge of town before he could fully acknowledge the truth, which was that he had not the slightest notion of where he was going or what, once he got there, he should hope to find.

But although perplexed, he could not blame himself again. By now he was weary of regret; he would not again say to himself that he had been presumptuous and foolish to stand for constable, that it would have been best to stay indoors and keep shop, satisfied that an honest clothier stands as nigh to God as a great lord or the old Queen herself. He had heaped enough ashes upon his head. Yet his commission still lay heavily upon his stomach, like too much beef eaten the night before.

At least, he thought as he walked, the country air might do him some good, might clear his head. Methodically, he inventoried the handful of facts he had established. It was not much of a store. The hostler's story was not beyond suspicion. Richard Mull's motives remained obscure, as did, certainly, the part Sir Henry and his lady might play in all of this. He had first discounted Joan's suspicions; now he was beginning to take them more seriously. And what of the poor girl drowned?

When he looked up from his musings, he found that he was not far from the inn. Ahead he could see its tall chimneys curling smoke in the brisk morning air. He lengthened his stride, coming atop the rise just as Simon appeared leading the roan mare from the stable toward the field. The hostler did not stop when Matthew hailed him, but led the mare on stolidly, his head to the ground as though it were the end of day rather than a beginning.

At the second call, the hostler looked up, his lips twisted into a sneer, his eyes blank and hostile.

"You are fortunate, Master Stock, that your cloth sells itself. Some of God's creatures must work."

The man's surly manner rankled Matthew, who prided himself on his even temper, but he ignored the hostler's remark, proceeding with the same questions as before. Simon kept walking the mare until they reached the pasture; then, with a slap on its rump, he sent the horse galloping off. The two men sat down on some stones.

"I have told you what I know," the hostler grumbled.

"True enough," Matthew replied, "but rehearsing your tale might bring something else to mind."

Simon cleared his throat and stared sullenly at his hobnail shoes. Mechanically, he began to repeat his story, explaining again how he followed Richard Mull and the scullery maid into the pasture, how Richard had encountered the stranger, and how the stranger and the boy had gone off together into the wood. The hostler said, "I did not hear what 'twas spoken. I did not see the stranger's face. I did not see 'em go."

Matthew examined the haggard face, taking the measure of the man's honesty as he might have judged a customer's ability to pay an account. The looks of the hostler were mean, rife with repressed violence, but they were no more so than those marking every third man's face, driven down with low wages and high costs. Yet Matthew knew this man was lying, or, at best, telling only part of the truth.

Matthew asked Simon to show him where the horses had been tethered. The two men trudged across the pasture. The ground was still soft from rain. They entered the trees, a forlorn, desolate spot out of sight of the inn and one Matthew could well imagine as the scene of a murder, especially at night before the moon had risen.

"Just here," Simon said, pointing to a clump of bushes. "The horses stood there. The boy and the man stood here."

Matthew sent the hostler back to his work and waited until Simon had crossed the pasture to the stable before beginning to examine the area. He poked around the bushes and grass, but without success. He could find no evidence of men or of horses. Then thinking the hostler might have been mistaken in the exact spot, the constable began to widen his search, and it was not long until he found a place where the grass had indeed been trampled and there was a confusion of prints in the moist ground. He thought, there must have been a struggle. Then, a short distance away, he saw the cloth, hanging from the branch of a hawthorn like a signal flag. He waded through the weeds to the hawthorn and plucked the cloth from the branch. It was a man's shirt, of good cambric and splendid silk needlework. The shirt had been ripped to shreds and was stained with blood. Matthew threw it aside. He knew whose shirt it had been. He was standing on the very spot the players' boy had been murdered.

Matthew looked about him, trembling. There was a flat gray sky, not a breath of wind, an eerie stillness that made him sick at heart. He recalled old stories about the spirits of murdered men. How those spirits haunted the places where the murders had occurred. He crossed himself and whispered a prayer. Then he began to move quickly through the damp grass toward the pasture.

His foot kicked against something and he bent down to pick it up. It was a piece of fine-tooled leather, stirrup leather from a gentleman's saddle, the iron lost somewhere. It could not have been there long in the grass. Matthew could smell yet the saddler's oil, feel a hostler's care. He looked again at the trampled earth, the signs of struggle, and his imagination reconstructed the scene: a sudden, sharp thrust, probably from behind and while the boy was off balance mounting the horse and unsuspecting, the horses startled by the violence, by the blood, lurching wildly. In the darkness the murderer or murderers had not noticed the damaged saddle, eager to be off and away as Matthew was now, from this unhallowed place.

He wiped the mud from the leather and examined it more closely. yes, there was something there, an ornately carved initial now that he looked more closely. The letter *S*. "Saltmarsh," the constable said aloud, as though someone had whispered it into his ear.

He folded the leather strap carefully and placed it inside his cloak.

Big Tod could hardly bear to sleep in the stable since the boy's death. He could not look into the straw but he saw Richard Mull's body. Sometimes he saw it out of the corner of his eye in odd places, propped up in the drinking room of the inn or smiling whimsically from behind the privy. The visions always made him shudder and cross himself, although of religion he had little, believing rather that when a man died that was the end of it. Had he been of a philosophical bent, he would have recognized the incompatibility of his visions and his opinions. But though he had a good heart and merry countenance, he was no philosopher, so he kept his visions and his opinions. And he slept restlessly.

He had awakened late, long after the crow of the cock. He lay thinking in the straw, thinking of the Welsh girl and her story. He had liked the maid; she had a pleasant wit and a ready smile. He had talked with her easily, as though they had been reared by the same hearth. He wanted to see her again—and safe from the dangers at the Hall.

His brother emitted a loud snore and started from sleep. Then the two went off to the inn in search of breakfast.

They were seated together at the window when Big Tod saw the constable approaching from the stable.

" 'Tis the constable, indeed," Little Tod said when his brother had called his attention to the window. "Let's greet him on our feet."

The brothers stood and walked toward the fire, Big Tod stretching himself to his full height. They nodded to the little constable when he entered. The innkeeper looked into the room and called out for the order.

Matthew said, "How soon will you be leaving us?"

"Sir Henry and his lady leave Friday for London. There is nothing for us here."

"You will travel to London with them?" Matthew asked.

"For that you must ask our chief," Big Tod replied. "I know not his plans, nor do I have any for myself."

When the innkeeper returned with the ale, Matthew took it firmly in hand and drank deep to warm his bones. Finding the strap had given him confidence, as disturbing as this evidence was. These two men, he thought, might be outlanders, and yet they were much like the folk he knew in Chelmsford and who knew him. "Would you mind if I joined you at your table for a bit?"

Big Tod motioned the constable to their table by the window. The table was narrow and their glasses nearly touched at its center.

"You have been many times to the Hall?"

"Twice," Big Tod replied laconically, hoisting his glass for a long drink that seemed to imply the sufficiency of his answer.

"Once last night. The other time four days before," Big Tod volunteered.

"Why ask you that?" the younger brother asked suspiciously.

Matthew examined the players shrewdly. "I ask because if I am to resolve Sir Henry's doubts in the boy's death I must know all of his doings. I know that Richard Mull was at the Hall more than twice."

"If 'tis true," Big Tod began, "you have the advantage of me, for he was there four days since, and that to my knowing was his one visit."

Undaunted, Matthew continued. "You know nothing then of any relation the boy may have had with Lady Salt-marsh?"

The question evidently caught the player by surprise. He hesitated before responding. Perhaps the constable was not such a great fool after all. He was tempted now to share what the Welsh girl had told him, but his oath of silence suppressed the inclination.

"I do not know what you mean by relation." He proceeded cautiously. "She was our patron, remains so still, she and her husband. Both favored the boy above the rest of us. I know no more."

He rose to leave, but the constable stayed him with a hand on his arm. "You seem an honest man. I should be much grieved were I to find you otherwise. Are you certain you know no more than you have told?"

"Of myself, I know no more than I have said just now. My brother and I must be about our business."

Big Tod followed his brother from the room into the courtyard, just as Will Shipman was emerging from the stable and making his own way to the inn for breakfast.

"The constable is inside," Big Tod remarked in passing the chief player.

Will Shipman nodded as he stepped into the room. The brothers proceeded to the stable in silence and began to collect their belongings. Big Tod was thinking of the Welsh girl again, but was uncertain as to what to do next.

Matthew had paused at the table until the brothers had gone out into the innyard. Through an open window he could see Will Shipman buttoning his jerkin and making his way to breakfast. The chief player had passed the brothers, nodding to them in greeting. There was little surprise on his face when he entered the inn and saw the constable standing at the bar.

Matthew greeted the chief player cheerfully. He was tempted to question the man again but suddenly thought the better of it. If he could not penetrate the silence of the brothers, he would do little better with Will Shipman. These actors kept close tongues.

He paid for his ale and walked out into the yard. He looked at the sky. There would be rain before nightfall.

He spent the hour's walk from the inn to the Hall fingering the strap in his pocket and munching his breakfast. The cheese was good but the biscuits stale. He could blame only himself; Joan had offered him hot caudle and pudding had he had the patience for it.

Zerubbabel Edwards was tall, muscular, and stood at the present moment working shirtless at the forge, a grumpy, recalcitrant fellow Matthew knew by reputation. When the constable identified himself over the din of anvil and hammer, the groom stared at Matthew suspiciously, and then continued his work, paying the constable no more mind than he would have a traveling tinker selling crocks and wooden spoons.

Matthew tried to get the man's attention again. Finally, the groom stopped. Beads of moisture trickled from his dark face onto his chest. He lowered the hammer and placed it on the anvil.

Matthew showed the groom the strap he had found. Edwards examined it, grunted something under his breath. " 'Tis my master's, indeed. How came you by it?"

"I found it in the road, on my way here," Matthew said, not yet prepared to describe his find as evidence. "You are sure though that it is truly Sir Henry's?"

"He has two saddles so marked. One for his gelding, one for his lady's. I should know well enough, for I care for his horses and their trappings."

"I'll give the piece to Sir Henry myself," Matthew declared reaching for it. But the groom tucked it into his belt.

"No need," he said. "It can be repaired. Sir Henry will not even know it was gone."

The man resumed hammering. Matthew noticed the man's brawny arms and shoulders and decided against pressing his authority, at least for the moment. Dejectedly, he bid the groom good day, not waiting a response from one who now seemed totally absorbed in his task. Matthew emerged from the stable at the exact moment Big Tod stepped from the kitchen of the Hall and stood in the distance talking to the Welsh girl. Matthew paused, watching the pair. Then he saw the actor take the girl in his arms, kiss her, and walk off in the direction of the road.

"I have thought of little but you since last night," Big Tod said.

"Nor I of you," Gwen replied simply.

He led her to the table in the kitchen where they had drunk together. They were alone in the great room with its immense unenclosed hearth and soot-stained rafters.

She leaned toward him and whispered hoarsely. "There was a terrible to-do last night between my master and his lady. When I came to bed I heard them below in their chamber, him screaming and pounding at her door."

"Could you not hear the matter?" he asked.

"Only their raging. My mistress's voice was shrill, angrier than I had before heard it. Sir Henry was drunk blind. Daniel the servingman told me so when he came into the kitchen from quenching the candles in the hall. He told me to be wary of the master, for he was muttering 'gainst women beneath his breath, and since I was surely one, that I might well watch where I stepped that night. Daniel helped the master to his chamber but waited at the door. The quarrel between them began no sooner than the door was shut and went on until much later. I went to bed myself where I sleep up beneath the rafters. After the moon had gone down I heard Sir Henry stumbling on the stairs and thought it might be Mary Dill, the upstairs maid, coming back from her husband's farm. She's fat and her footfall's like unto a man's. But then I heard him snorting, so I knew it was the master himself. He reeked of vomit. I could smell it through the door. I heard him feeling around in the darkness and then he bumped his shins on my bedpost and cursed. I was frightened out of my wits but kept still, hoping that he'd not find me. Then he touched my leg, and I let out a little scream. He grabbed for my throat, so that I

96

could hardly breathe, and told me to keep quiet or I'd scream for the devil anon.''

"Sure he is the devil himself," Big Tod interjected angrily.

"He told me that I was a goodly wench, spoke sweetly to me. How I was a wench a lord might wish to keep his bed warm in the winter, but that if I was as quick with my tongue as with my nose that they'd bury me before the first snow.''

"Ah, then he did see you the day you interrupted his wife's pleasure?''

"Aye, I think he did, but he did not speak of that. I concluded that it was not my silence about what had happened was his interest but what he was about to do, for he handled me most unmannerly, feeling such parts of me that I am ashamed to tell of it, and roughly too.''

Big Tod's anger mounted. "I've a knife that I'd find a sweet home for in the seat of his lust, the great devil. Did he do you harm?''

"Nay, I'm a virgin still, but not for his want of trying. God, I was most sick with the smell, but he floundered about the bed like a great fish beached. I lay still, corpselike, which made him angry at first, but I was too busy keeping my own gorge down to feign the passion he desired. Soon he tired of me and lay gasping, then began to snore. I lay quiet as could be and then pushed him to the side and got out of bed as fast as I might.''

"And what did you then?''

"I ran as fast to where the menservants sleep, woke Daniel, and told him that the master had stumbled to my bed and asked him to see to him. I waited while Daniel went about the business. When he returned he told me that he had helped Sir Henry to his own chamber below but that my mistress would give him no admittance, though both Sir Henry and Daniel pleaded. So Daniel found a place for Sir Henry in one of the guest chambers. Like enough it suited him, such a state he was in.''

"Like enough," Big Tod said stonily.

Gwen continued. "I returned to my own room but could not sleep in a bed so foul. I was more angry than afraid by that time to think that on my pittance I must endure such as this.''

Big Tod shook his head sympathetically and reached for her hand.

"But that was not the whole of it," she said. "This morning as I was cleaning up after cook, my mistress came into the kitchen and beckoned me toward the garden. She asked me to tell her of what passed last night, which I truthfully did. I guess she had wheedled from Daniel in whose bed he had found Sir Henry, and she, guessing why, was looking hard into my honesty. Strangely, it took me no trouble to satisfy her of that, but then she put more direct warnings to me touching upon the minding of my own business in the Hall and how I would be treated if I carried tales into the town."

"Did she say aught of the other time?"

"Nay, except that she did talk somewhat shadowily of things I might have seen and must not relate to a living soul. These were Sir Henry's private business, she said, then looked as though she wished me dead. I spoke up and assured her that I could keep silent and knew my place and was a simple maid who wished only to earn her keep in an honest way."

"How did that satisfy her, then?"

"Well, she said no more but turned and went back into the house. So of my situation here now I can say no more."

" 'Tis a dangerous thing when a serving girl must keep silent for her master and his lady, for though she be as discreet as a log, should her master become suspicious it will be small time before evil befalls her."

She shuddered and drew closer to him. He had not meant to alarm her, and yet he knew too much of what men were capable of to overlook these signs of danger. He pressed her hands reassuringly. "Come with me now, child," he said. "The danger grows greater should you stay."

"But I have not my things," she protested.

"What you need I will provide myself," he said. "Let me return to my chamber for my mother's locket." she said, "which I have concealed beneath my bed. 'Tis precious little I have to remember her by, and she willed it specially to me. I cannot leave it in good conscience.''

"Go then and be quick," he said sharply. "I'll wait you beyond the porter's lodge. Tell no one of your leaving and make no fuss. If any ask, say that you have been sent to town on an errand, for thread or some bauble. Carry a basket with you. 'Twill make the tale all the more likely.''

She signaled her understanding with a quick nod and then disappeared into the passageway connecting the kitchen with the great hall. He rose and stepped out into the courtyard. Seeing no one, he began to walk quickly toward the lodge.

Varnell followed the Welsh girl up the back staircase to her chamber in the attic and watched while she rummaged through the bed linens, stuffed something—into her bosom, and then turned suddenly to see him standing over her. She gasped; he barred her way from the room with an arm across the door.

"You'll not hurt me?" she asked, her face ashen with fear.

He dropped his arm but did not move from the doorway. "You mistake me," he said. "I mean you no harm, but you must come with me now to Sir Henry."

He took her hand and led her firmly from the room as a parent might lead a disobedient child. Below he waited with her outside the knight's door until they were bidden to enter. He could feel the girl shudder; his own pulse quickened with excitement.

Saltmarsh scowled and let a heavy volume fall to his table with a thud that made her jump. His doublet was now clean and properly secured; he seemed a quite different man from the half-blind drunk who had come staggering into her chamber only a few hours before. The secretary withdrew at his master's command.

When he beckoned her to approach, she stood her ground timorously, then yielded. A lord in his cups, rutting for a maid, was just another drunken man who must be helped to the door or to his own bed. A knight sober was another beast. Though she dreaded both, this she knew was the worse.

"Daniel tells me that you have a loose tongue, girl. Is that true or no?" He spoke evenly, his tone almost casual.

"I know not what you might mean, sir," she replied hesitantly.

"You have told him that I came to your chamber yesternight to have . . . conversation with you, did you not? And I suppose you are now going to the town to relate the same to your gossips?" He seized her long hair in his fist and pulled it back sharply.

"I would do no such thing," she gasped in pain.

"You should not tell such a thing, for there is no truth in it, is there?"

To her relief, he released her hair and walked toward the window. She began to weep. He commanded, his back to her still, "Cease whimpering and tell me what you told Daniel, word for word."

She hesitated, controlled her tears, and decided to lie. Between sobs, she said, "I told him that you had come to my chamber, mistaking it for your own, and that he should come fetch you to see you to your proper bed, Sir Henry."

She waited to see the effect of this invention on the knight, but since she was unable to read the back of his head she could only surmise his reaction and pray that Daniel's more honest, if malicious, account had been vague enough to accommodate her own story.

Evidently it was, for Saltmarsh said nothing but continued to look out the window at the bleak fields. When he turned to her again, his heavy face had regained its usual expressionlessness. "Do you recall exactly what I said to you, word for word when I came to you?"

Now that he faced her, she could read the uncertainty in his eyes. So he was too drunk then to remember and it was her word against Daniel's. Well, she was content to stand her ground. If her master had said or done aught improper, then she could certainly not tell, for the hour was late, herself half asleep. That she could remember him entering her chamber at all was a wonder, much less the details of his discourse or actions.

He suffered her to reason thusly, saying nothing but continuing to scrutinize her with that same emotionless stare. When she was finished, she let her arms fall to her side.

"I deal harshly with servants who speak of what passes in this house out of it. You are a girl here by virtue of my wife's sufferance, not mine. For her sake I shall forgive what seems to have been an error—yours or Daniel's I cannot tell. Let the matter end in this, that though I may at times drink more than moderation allows, I observe the laws of God and man when it comes to the women of this house. No maid in my wife's service need fear me."

All this he pronounced with such frigid dignity that she could almost have thought herself mistaken in him. She blushed in spite of herself for shame, curtsied, and at his permission departed the chamber bewildered and frightened.

With the door fast behind her, she hurriedly returned to her own quarters and finished packing her belongings in the basket Big Tod had given her. In her mind's eye she saw him waiting her and wondering at her long delay, and she feared how he might misinterpret it as simple harlotry. She hoped he might think her done away with instead, and maybe weep for her rather than condemn. From her tiny window she peered down into the courtyard and saw Sir Henry's secretary standing idly by the gate looking up at her. Her heart sank. She was not our of danger yet. She gathered her cloak, first making sure the locket was secure in her bodice. Then she hurried down the passage to the back stairs, wishing to avoid the courtyard and the pasty-face secretary at all cost.

"You are waiting someone?" Matthew Stock said as, breathless but smiling, he caught up with the player at the lodge.

"Aye, the girl at the Hall. She and I have been friendly with one another and are thinking of marrying. That is, if there's none to say us nay."

"You shall find no objector in me, then." the constable returned pleasantly. "But what of Sir Henry?"

"I care not," Big Tod exploded. "She's no slave and may go as she pleases."

"Unless she is pledged or bound," Matthew reminded him.

"She is neither, but a free woman working for a wage."

"Then if such be the case, I wish you both Godspeed."

Matthew turned, as if to go on his way, and then stopped. "I am surprised that your amorous duties should have carried you so abruptly to the Hall following our conversation. Would you mind if I waited with you and spoke to the girl myself? She may know more of the doings here than any of us, and may provide useful information about the boy's murder."

The player knew the request admitted no denying. The two men waited together in silence. "The girl delays her coming," the constable said after a quarter of an hour had passed and there was yet no sign of her.

"Women will be ever long about their doings," Big Tod reflected philosophically, attempting to hide his growing unease.

"And that's the truth. But tell me, I wonder that you have persuaded the girl to leave so secure a place to wander England with your troop. I do not deny that you be a proper man, but women are homey folk not soon to leave a well-feathered nest."

"She has no one here," the player responded sullenly. "She longs for a different scene."

"And what said she about her mistress, pray?"

But the constable's question was pre-empted by the sight of the Welsh girl hurrying up the road. When she saw the two men standing together, she stopped abruptly, as though puzzled, then she continued on toward them.

Matthew had paid the girl little mind when he had first seen her in the hall. Now he observed in her expression a fierce determination and concern which gave the simple lines of her face a more womanly character. He noticed that when they met the lovers did not embrace but stood awkwardly apart, the player with his thumbs inserted in his belt, and the maid clutching the basket she carried as though it were a newborn child she was afraid to drop.

Big Tod spoke first. "You have come at last, and about time, too."

The girl said nothing. Matthew could now see that her eyes were red and swollen from weeping. The player continued: "I have told the constable here of our wedding plans, so he knows we are about to leave this place. But he would still have some words with you before we may be on our way."

"The wind is turning cold again," Matthew said. "Let us walk toward the hedge to do our talking. I do know that you have merry business before you and would not impede its progress. I promise I shall make quick work of my words."

the three walked a short distance to where a hedge of oak and hawthorn broke the monotony of the fields. Matthew began directly, determining her origin, her conduct in the house, and her reason for leaving Lady Saltmarsh's employ. At the last question she hesitated, and then Big Tod burst in to reaffirm their betrothal. Matthew could read no denial in her face, only an uneasiness which he took as a sign of her eagerness to be off.

"Were you much in her ladyship's company?" Matthew said.

"I was her maid. My duties were to look after her linen, to help her to dress and undress, to empty the chamber pot each morning, and fetch whatever was wanted from below."

The constable decided to phrase his next question carefully. "Did you ever see her with the players' boy, Richard Mull?"

A look of astonishment crossed the girl's face. Now he was certain he had found something. Without giving her a chance to respond, he honed his question to an even finer point.

"Did you ever find Richard Mull and your mistress in close company?"

"I do not know what you mean, sir," she replied weakly.

"I mean," Matthew explained patiently, "did you ever

observe that her fondness for the boy was what it ought not to have been?''

The girl and player exchanged glances. In the man's expression, Matthew thought he detected a warning.

'' 'Tis not a maid's place to pry into her mistress's business,'' the girl replied, her eyes to the ground. ''If my lady did aught but what would please her husband, I know it not.''

At this, Big Tod took up her cause. ''You can see, Constable, that her mind is elsewhere now. She is an honest girl, not one to carry tales or pry. Now we best be on our way.''

Matthew looked at the two standing before him. They seemed after all a likely couple. Indeed, they reminded him of Joan and himself before their own marriage years before. He decided not to delay them with more questions. ''I thank you for what you have said, and wish Godspeed to both. May you be as happy as my wife and me these twenty years.''

The three walked toward the road together and were bidding farewell again when they heard the horsemen coming across the fields. Matthew turned to see Saltmarsh's secretary astride one of the horses and the surly groom, Zerubbabel Edwards, on the other.

Varnell shouted at them to stand, and reined in his horse sharply. ''Hold the girl,'' he said.

''By whose command?'' Big Tod responded angrily.

''I would put to you the same question, Master Secretary,'' Matthew said. ''Is the girl not free then?''

''She's not, but bound for five years, only two of which she has served.''

Matthew looked to the girl, whose face was blank with terror. ''Is what the man says true, girl, are you bound?''

The girl stood speechless, bent over and suddenly old. He walked toward her and pried her hand loose from the player's arm. Big Tod stared at the ground dejectedly.

''I have no choice but to surrender you to your lawful master. Such is the law,'' Matthew said.

The words brought Big Tod back to life. He grabbed the girl and looked threateningly at the other men. ''She shall not go with you," he thundered, his right hand firmly on the dagger at his side.

"You will keep the peace," Matthew Stock said firmly, seeing the groom on the point of drawing his own blade.

He turned to look at the Welsh girl and the player. "Do either of you wish now to tell me if there be any reason why the girl should fear to return to the Hall?"

The girl began to weep, Big Tod pulled her to him protectively. The groom glowered and unsheathed a sword, while the big player looked as if he would need little urging to throttle the man had he the chance.

"These two," Matthew began in an official tone, "I arrest and charge with resistance to an officer of the law and breaking the peace. You two interfere at your peril, for though she be runaway, my charge takes the precedence of Sir Henry's. As for you, my man," Matthew continued, looking sternly toward the groomsman, "I will leave you for Master Varnell to rule. See to it that Sir Henry knows of this. I will present these two to him tomorrow with my charge."

Varnell and the groom exchanged glances but made no further show of force. Then the secretary pulled up on his reins and the two rode away.

The girl began to weep again. Matthew said, "That's the last we'll see of that pair today. Tomorrow may be a different story. Come now with me. Your arrest is no jest. My wife and I will find a place for you beside our fire."

9

JOAN'S nimble fingers plied her needle until the ornate filigree of lace was done. Then she examined her work with satisfaction and laid it aside, her eyelids half closed as though heavy with sleep.

But she was not asleep, not even drowsy. She had been thinking about the murder, and the more she thought the more confused she became. A good housewife, she had a passion for neatness; she would have put the world in order had she the doing of it within her power. But everything to do with Richard Mull and his dreadful death was askew in her mind. She envisioned it all as though it were an array of tragic scenes like the pageant wagons she had seen as a child on holidays, each one with its own dramatized story. She could not connect the sordid murder with the finery of the Hall, Richard Mull with Cecilia Saltmarsh, the horrible hostler with Sir Henry, the dandified secretary and the priest with the dark eyes and long face. Yet she was sure that somewhere at the hall the motive for Richard Mull's death squatted like a toad half buried in the muddy bottom of a pond.

Determining the motive, she realized, depended on making sense of relationships—what the boy had been to Sir

Henry, what to his lady. Cecilia Saltmarsh was a young woman, beautiful and polished. Perhaps she had grown weary of her husband's neglect and had taken the young actor as her lover. Perhaps Sir Henry had discovered the same and ordered the boy's death. Or, she speculated further, Lady Saltmarsh herself might have been the offended party. She may have found the boy unfaithful with another—perhaps the girl at the inn—and given commands. Great ladies, she knew, had often done as much. Jealousy might enrage a saint.

Then her imagination shaped events in another way. What if Sir Henry had lusted after the boy himself? The idea was repugnant to her. It would never have occurred to her had the play not suggested it as she watched the aged Jupiter dandle Ganymede upon his knee. Sir Henry may have promoted the entertainment of the players so that he might be nearer to his unnatural love. Perhaps the boy refused outright—or perhaps he complied. Either response might provoke a murder, she thought, especially had the boy threatened to reveal the knight's passion.

Presently these fancies dissolved; she discarded them as simple and perverse. She felt guilty for even thinking them, as though the very idea of the act tainted her own soul. Besides, she thought, country knights might find easier ways to undo their rivals than making a public spectacle of their private affairs, especially if the knight were also magistrate. Such, she had heard, worked much by poison, always had their murders done by other hands, and paid well that their victims' bodies were never found or, if so, not to be distinguished from poor folk died of the fever and unburied. It also came hard to her to think of how such a tall man as Sir Henry was to come to play the cuckold to a stripling, hardly man enough to give a grown woman pleasure.

She retreated from this particular line of thought as she might have withdrawn in distaste from the sight of a fly-blown cat before her door.

The man who entered at that moment with her husband she recognized as one of the players. At his side was a thin girl of about her daughter's age with dark features twisted with apprehension and fear. She might be fair, Joan thought, had her mouth been shaped by another humor. At once she thought of the player and the girl as a pair, an impression immediately confirmed by her husband, who introduced them as betrothed, but only after he first somewhat awkwardly inquired of the girl her name. She was Gwen Mair of Carmarthen.

Joan said, "You are far from home, child."

"I have taken this man and maid into custody," Matthew was saying, motioning them both to chairs by the fire. "To keep them out of the Hall for the night. On the morrow they may be about their own business."

"Why, what have they done, pray?" Joan asked with sudden alarm, for she wanted no felons within her door, no matter how innocent the two might appear by their faces.

"It is but a stratagem," Matthew explained matter-of-factly, removing his cloak and making himself comfortable by the fire. "Peter Varnell and the groom from the Hall tried to force the girl to return, saying she was a runaway. They came upon us with horses. But if she can prove she is free and clear, they'll have no cause to hold her."

"Aye, and she can so prove," Big Tod said, speaking for the first time since they had entered the room.

"If so, nothing more will come of it. You'll be safe here tonight. Tomorrow you may be on your way." Matthew called for Betty, who led the couple to the spare bedchamber above.

"Now, my husband," Joan said, "pray tell what has happened since you left me so downcast this morning. You seem lively enough now."

Matthew placed another log on the fire and resumed his chair opposite Joan's. He began to relate his discovery. Joan listened with interest, interrupting him occasionally with a question or exclamation.

"The piece of leatherwork I found was from one of Sir Henry's saddles. It bore his initial, carved skillfully into the leather.

"Then it was Sir Henry's horses in the wood," she concluded.

"Indeed, his horses, but who was the stranger? That's the question."

"Well at least you have connected the murder with the Hall and that's a great thing."

"Save that I no longer have the evidence. Stupidly I allowed the groom to have it and was of no stomach to demand its return, not without the watch behind me."

Matthew and Joan watched the fire grow great on the hearth and then decline. Later Big Tod and Gwen joined them in a simple supper. Gwen ate but a speak of meat, but Big Tod consumed a whole capon and much ale to wash it down. Danger seemed to have made him ravenous. Joan sought to draw Gwen out of her gloom with cheery proverbs or recollections of her own young womanhood, but Gwen sat pensive, her mind full of dark images.

When supper was done, the four gathered by the kitchen fire and after each was seated comfortably close Matthew began his questions:

"Today when I asked you about affairs at the Hall you told me nothing. I knew then your silence was out of fear, and though you are fearful still you are now among friends who wish you well."

Gwen turned her blue eyes toward the constable and shifted uneasily in her chair. Big Tod extended his hand and gave hers an encouraging pat.

"Tell Master Stock what you told me," Big Tod urged gently.

Gwen looked up at him, not so much out of reluctance to speak as from uncertainty as to how to begin.

"Aye, about what you saw with your mistress and the boy—and about Sir Henry too."

Then the girl, her eyes fixed upon the fire as though in a trance, related to them all what she had previously told Big Tod.

Varnell grimaced, mopped the sweat from his brow, and sent the groom to see to the horses. He knew Sir Henry would not take his failure lightly; but then, he considered, he would not have made matters better had he rushed the constable and taken the girl by force. Besides, he saw no need to risk breaking his skull in a fight.

He found Saltmarsh alone, sitting comfortably with a book. "You have brought the girl?" the knight asked without lifting his eyes from the page.

The secretary's voice trembled uncontrollably. "We were prevented, sir. The constable and one of the players made bold resistance. We feared to shed blood on such slight grounds."

"The constable made resistance?" Saltmarsh asked incredulously.

"Indeed, sir. He held that his own charge of their breaking the Queen's peace took precedence above yours. He has taken both of them into custody and boasts that he will keep them there until tomorrow when he can determine the truth of the girl's condition."

Saltmarsh shoved the book aside and walked angrily to the window. Peter Varnell shuddered, relieved to find his employer's wrath directed to some other person. After several moments of silence, Saltmarsh said simply, "You may go. Mind you, Master Varnell, learn courage of some woman. You have much need of such before you can serve me."

Stung to the quick, Peter Varnell bowed cringingly. "I shall study as you direct," he said, feeling his way from the room as though his eyesight were obscured by a heavy mist.

When the door was closed behind him, he suppressed a curse and nursed his confusion by gnawing upon his thumb until the pain brought him to his senses. He turned abruptly and made for Cecilia Saltmarsh's chamber.

The new girl admitted him, plump and ruddy-faced and new enough still in the house to treat him with proper fear. She ushered him into the bedchamber where Varnell found the mistress of Saltmarsh Hall reclining on her bed. The lady greeted him, and he came quickly to his point. "You asked me lately if I were willing to be of service to you— You wanted to know about the boy, and said you would reward me as I deserved. Do you still hold to that?"

"That would depend," she said eyeing him curiously. She dismissed the girl, rose from the bed, and invited him to sit. "Now speak, Master Varnell, what have you?"

He spoke hurriedly, still so enraged at Saltmarsh that he cared nothing for the consequences. "Your husband commanded the boy's murder. He ordered me to hire the hostler to the work. I went to the inn as I have done before to fetch the boy. He came willingly, suspecting nothing more than the prospect of your entertainment. When we arrived where I had left the horses, the hostler sprang from his place of concealment, seized the boy about the neck, and dispatched him. It was over quickly. I helped the hostler carry the body back to the stable. When the players retired there later they were too weary or drunk to find anything but their own beds in the straw."

Varnell paused, breathless. Cecilia Saltmarsh's face was white, she groaned a little, and then looked at Varnell with a steady gaze.

"I speak God's truth." he said.

"I have no doubt of that. 'Tis too simple and likely to be otherwise."

She sighed heavily and walked to her window. For a while she said nothing. Varnell waited, not daring to open his mouth again. Then she said, "You have confessed to murder, Master Varnell. What am I to think? I would ask you why you did it, but it would be a vain question. Yet now that I consider it, why should I believe *all* of what you have said? My husband commanded the death? You say that indeed, but how can I be sure that you did not conceive what you have just now admitted to have executed. You've wedged yourself into a narrow place, Master Secretary. A confessed murderer, now wishing to implicate his master? What proof have you that you and the hostler acted on my husband's orders and not out of your own malice?"

She looked at him strangely. Varnell shuddered and his heart began to race again. He tried to think clearly. What proof *was* there? Saltmarsh had suborned him privately with an account of the knight's motives to which Varnell had given but a single ear, since the secretary had detested the boy already and was glad to be of use anyway. Something about a husband's jealousy and a wife's indiscretion. Plausible enough, Varnell had thought; and the act had not

111

offended his own conscience since the hostler was to strike the actual blow, not Varnell.

"I wonder," she said icily, "that you should so traduce your master as to convey to his wife such a wicked story as this to cover your own crime."

"My lady—"

"Indeed—and your master's wife."

Her eyes blazed with anger. Varnell sat stunned, struggling to hold back tears and shaking uncontrollably. He protested, "I never intended . . . I thought you had no great love for your husband—"

"You thought—!" She turned abruptly. Varnell remained seated, not daring to move. When she turned again, her face seemed transformed. There was no anger visible, only a steady gaze of contempt. Varnell withered under it. He wished himself dead in his grave.

"Get out."

He didn't move; his legs wouldn't move.

"I said, get out. My husband will know of this."

"Please, lady—"

"Nothing you could say or do will please me now. You have betrayed your master with this false account and betrayed me as well in thinking I should so wish to know of my husband's private affairs as to procure your service."

"I'll take my leave, then," he managed to say. His mouth was dry, as though he had not drunk for a week. His heart beat violently and he could feel beads of sweat upon his brow even though the chamber was cold.

He stumbled from the room, blind with fear, bumping into the serving girl who had been waiting outside the chamber. The girl looked up at him with wide eyes and seeing the terror in his face shrunk from him. He pushed her aside and started down the passageway, not sure where he would go, when he heard Cecilia Saltmarsh call. He stopped and turned. His mistress was standing there staring after him. Her face had changed again; to his amazement she seemed unmoved, calm, as though their interview had been a dream from which he had now awakened. She beckoned him to return to her. "Perhaps I have misjudged you," she said softly. She glared at the girl, who quickly ran off, and Varnell followed Cecilia Saltmarsh back into her bedchamber.

"If you had some proof," she said. "The hostler, you say, was your fellow in this?"

Varnell admitted it again.

"Did you tell him that Richard's death was my husband's will?"

Varnell could not remember, but he said yes. He knew he would say anything now. His terror was subsiding, but he was still confused, dizzy with the sudden changes in her manner and sick at heart. He did not know whether to smile agreeably or keep sober and repentent. He wondered if he were walking into another trap, but he did not know how to begin to avoid it. Whichever way he went lay danger. He said, "I would offer you proof indeed if there were aught, but the work was planned in secret and so executed."

She looked thoughtful, then she went to a cabinet in the corner of the room, withdrew a small chest, and returned with five gold coins in her hand. "Here," she said. "Keep four for yourself and give the fifth to the hostler.

"Bring him here. If he confirms what you have said, then I will believe it true and hold you in my heart as a trusted friend. If not, then I will advise my husband of what tales you bear to his wife. I trust he will find another secretary speedily enough."

"And if the hostler will not come?"

"Give him the coin only if he does, and take an extra horse with you that you may lose no time in coming and going."

"I will, my lady."

"And, Master Varnell," she said as she returned to her bed, "the gold you may consider only partial payment in this business. I may have other work for you as well, but only if you prove honest in this."

"Believe me, lady, I will prove so, for I would rather serve you than God."

She laughed huskily at his wit, complimented him on his new satin suit, and bid him Godspeed. "Do not be impious," she called after him. "It is sufficient that you serve me."

He gave her one final awkward bow and stumbled from the room, still so shaken and bewildered by the variation in her response to him that he did not know whether to feel gratitude or smoldering hate. He had blurted out his part in the murder in a moment of anger—for revenge. He had nearly had himself hanged! What a fool he had been to lose his temper thus. On the other hand, his mistress obviously wished to know the truth. More, she was willing to pay a price for it, and he might yet get something out of that worth the hell he had gone through.

"I can scarce credit it," Matthew said with wonder when Gwen had finished her story. "The husband a willing witness to his own cuckolding! Had Joan done such, I would have killed the man and probably her after, though I love her as my life."

"Richard Mull went often to the Hall," Big Tod explained. "I told you not before because I feared it might put us into trouble with Sir Henry. He and his lady are our only patrons. We could little afford their displeasure."

"God must judge such conduct," Joan said in a whisper, looking to her husband for affirmation of her horror.

"In faith, 'tis so," Matthew agreed solemnly. "But this only complicates my charge. For how am I to bring to justice him who administers it?"

The four exchanged glances of bewilderment while the firelight played fantastically upon their faces. Big Tod said, "Of the law I know little, but surely even the magistrate must be accountable for his deeds. If this deed be proved, then 'tis Sir Henry himself who must stand tall for it. If he did not himself slit young Richard's belly, he paid for the act from his own pocket."

"Aye, that's it," Joan said, shaking her head. "The proof is what is needed. At the motive we may but guess, for we have come upon a well of evil and there's no sounding the bottom."

Matthew turned to his wife. In the firelight, half of her face fell into shadows like the moon. Huddled together, they all looked like conspirators, their faces intent and solemn, planning some desperate enterprise.

"From the beginning, Joan, you have had the best nose in this business. I know not if it be woman's wit that has led you to it, but as for now, I am tempted to trust you for the remainder. What think you now?"

She sat awhile pensively; she did not acknowledge her husband's compliment, although she was grateful for it. She was pleased to be taken so seriously but half afraid of the attention upon her. Seeing in Gwen's face a look of concern, she patted the girl's hand reassuringly. She said, " 'Tis not witchcraft, child. I love God and wish no powers beyond those other mortals have. But since my husband has fallen heir to this business, I have had inklings and seen them confirmed too when we went to the Hall and saw Sir Henry's play. I knew then that she was no happy wife. She carried herself like a woman seeking more than purity of heart allows. From time to time I read her glances. Trust me that those glances bore no good will toward her husband. You have helped us to know the cause, for 'twould seem neither husband nor wife follows the natural course, but the one is given to dark sins of which honest folk know not even the names."

"I know this about the law," Matthew added when his wife had done. "And that is that proof is what's wanted. Although none of us doubts who is guilty, neither do we know the why of it, or his agent, and that must be uncovered before justice may be done—in the court of men at least. But now the hour is late, though sleep may come hard to us, considering what we have said here."

That they took as a signal to bid each other good night. Big Tod and Gwen went to where their lodging had been assigned, Big Tod to bed with the apprentices, Gwen to find a warm place with Alice and Betty.

"I fear I was not made to be constable, Joan," Matthew said with a yawn when he was already deep within their bed. She climbed in beside him and crept close.

"No man is made but to be a man. For his calling in this life we must look to other causes."

"Always the philosopher, Joan," he said sleepily. "You

should have been such, had it lain in a woman's way. Your life has been wasted as a mere wife.''

"A mere wife, you say?" She sat upright in bed, feigning outrage. "No mere wife manages your affairs with the skill that I do, keeping a house such as this with two lazy louts as Alice and Betty be and five unruly apprentices to chase from the buttery every quarter of an hour.''

Then she said more seriously to her husband, who had already turned upon his side and shut his eyes, "You have done your best. Cats may see in the dark, but we know well what company they keep. You are a good man, Matthew. Your ways are straight as God or any wife should wish. I would rather have them so than you a speedier discoverer of wrongdoing.''

But he had fallen asleep. His breath came heavily and his eyelids fluttered as they did when he dreamed.

10

WHEN the priest awoke, light was already filtering through the windowpane and he could hear rain falling steadily on the roof. He had forgotten how dismal England could be in October. His heart sank, and he wished he were in France again.

Remembering poor Marlowe's death, even after eight years, had set the tone for this present mood. He found his boots beneath the bed and put them on. Then he stepped across the floor to the closet, where he retrieved the better of his two suits. He examined his face in the glass. He had shaved yesterday. The stubble was just beginning to show and he would not have to shave until tomorrow.

He used the chamber pot, from which the acrid smell of stale urine rose, and then placed the pot outside his chamber door for the girl. There was no water for washing.

He dressed quickly, making note of a missing button, and combed his hair. Then he sat down on his bed and waited.

He had pursued many women, and because they had found him handsome and clever he had always gotten what he wanted. He thought them lesser creatures than men. Their fragility and timidity proved that, and yet he allowed them their mystery, believing that as careful as his scrutiny of them had been there was more than met his eye. The present case proved as much. He had found Cecilia Saltmarsh's strategy of seduction beguiling though transparent, for he had ever considered the artfulness of sensuous woman fascinating even when their goal was his undoing. He was not sure that he had not been undone now. He had allowed her to have her way because he knew that it would bring them both to his. But as for the climax, he could have had more satisfaction from a dull country baggage who knew no more than to lie still and grit her teeth. Now his desire for her, long nurtured in his imagination since their first meeting in France, was quite as cold as his chamber.

He had accomplished, then, what he had come to the Hall to accomplish. He decided to leave quickly, if only to avoid seeing her again, and yet his curiosity as to which face she might put on for his benefit and her husband's almost overwhelmed him. Yes, he could wait.

When he heard a rap at his door he said come, thinking it the maid to change his bedding, but when he looked up to see his host himself he rose quickly.

"You have slept well, sir priest?" Henry Saltmarsh said curtly. He walked deliberately to the center of the chamber, his arms folded before him and his face set in what the priest might have interpreted as the beginning of a smile did the tone of voice not belie it.

"Sir Henry," he began awkwardly, "I thought not to find you outside or I would have risen to admit you."

"Say you?" Saltmarsh said icily.

The priest sensed danger and was silent. Saltmarsh paused, then proceeded in measured phrases as though he were reciting a litany. "You have abused my hospitality, sir, using my wife foully. I would not have tolerated that in a gentleman, much less in a scurvy priest."

"Sir Henry!" the priest gasped in astonishment.

"You deny it?"

The priest fell silent. Although disappointed with the lady's damp amorousness, he had thought he had at least taken accurate measure of her discretion.

118

"Has your lady said as much?" he protested weakly.

Saltmarsh turned his back on the priest contemptuously. "She has indeed told me of your rape. Were I not invested as magistrate, I might well do justice of my own with this sword."

"What did she tell you?" he asked incredulously.

Saltmarsh hesitated. "She told me that she came yesternight to your chamber for confession, that in the course of her prayers you did sue unto her. She refusing, you fell to her violently and despite her struggles you lay with her."

From the corner of his eye the priest caught a mouse scampering across the floor. He realized that the full truth would more likely enrage than appease Saltmarsh. He framed his features into remorse, using the thoughts of his own death as an impetus and the theatrical skill he had acquired as a player at Cambridge.

"What her ladyship says is most true," he began weakly. "Despite my vows, I was beguiled. Yesternight I thought nought but to hear her confession, but upon discovery of her humility and loveliness so openly displayed in her nightgown I was overcome with feelings I should never have permitted in my heart and I did lust after her. When she had confessed to me, I confessed my heart to her, but she would have none of my ardor, did in fact plea for a return of my sanity. She belittled her own beauty that it should incite me to such riot and lamented my loss of virtue. I took her by force. When she departed from me, I was overcome with remorse as I am still. I have prayed to God all the night for forgiveness."

"But you are now dressed. You have attained forgiveness, then?" Saltmarsh inquired cynically, walking toward the small window.

"I have not yet received forgiveness, and may not, save I am forgiven by both the man and woman I have wronged."

"Oh, then you seek my forgiveness, and that of my lady?" Saltmarsh mused.

"If it were possible; if not, 'twere better I were hanged, for in the death of my body for my crime I may yet hope to see my God."

Saltmarsh turned from the window and walked toward the priest, his arms at his side, his face fixed in the now familiar half smile, the intent of which the priest found quite impenetrable.

"Forgiving you is hardly compatible with my honor as a gentleman. You have abused my wife, there's no denying it. And yet you may partially redeem yourself in my eyes, and even in hers, should you be willing, and save yourself yet from the gibbet."

The priest grasped for the opening. "I would do anything, sir, to be restored to your and your lady's good graces, although I could hardly hope for such."

"I detest the act, despise it as a Christian and a gentleman, but your repentance pleases me well. Let me but think upon your crime the more and ways to redeem it. Your plans, I presume, will not take you from this house?"

Saltmarsh said this last with sufficient menace to make the priest quite sure of his own answer.

"They will not, sir. I stay but at your pleasure—and my lady's—hoping to secure your forgiveness and my God's."

When Saltmarsh had gone, the priest sat back down on the bed, his heart beating rapidly. The craven behavior to which he had been driven filled him with disgust. He played parts well, and could come on more priestly than the Pope should he choose; but he rarely liked the parts his present profession required of him. Besides, he reflected more calmly now, this country lordlet was doubtless a great devil himself with the ladies and one with more sins on his back than fish had scales. Well, his groveling had saved his own neck, at least for the time being. What Saltmarsh might have in mind in the way of redemption was at present beyond his imagining. Now he must bide his time and wait. It would not do to go running off, or the town constable would have yet another commission to grieve him—and one more easily executed than solving the player's murder of which he had heard in the town.

"So," she was saying, "you have spoken with the priest. And how did he respond to your threats? He denied all, I should think."

Fully clothed, her husband extended himself on her bed, his arms behind his head. "More warmly than you to his suit, my dear. Yet he kept his choler hidden well enough under as artful a humility as I have seen. He is fit company for you."

"But not for you?" she returned sharply.

"Well, perhaps. But in any case I played the outraged husband and he the fallen priest, and both with such skill that had we been on the London stage we should have brought a good penny to the house. When I accused him of rape, you would have thought he had consumed a live eel so pale did he become—and stuttered too, as though he had lost his teeth in the thicket of his beard. As for me, I put on a face of scarcely contained anger, adorned with the hint of a smile as you see me now—just so—so as to perplex him the more. I sent fear to his gut straightway."

She laughed dryly. "And did he fear? Did he grovel?"

"Oh, most assuredly. And he swore that he had been at prayers most of the night and had yet to gain forgiveness of his God. His God! Were there such, he would fall from high heaven with laughter at the scene."

She said, "You believe all men hypocrites because you wear many faces yourself. But some men, my husband, are honest. They wear but one face, their own, and it is enough for them."

Saltmarsh rose from the bed and walked to where she gazed at herself in the ornate mirror he had bought at Paris at considerable cost. Putting his arm around her shoulders, he said. "And what would you do, my lady, were I to wear but one face? What pleasure would that give you, for whom variety is as dear as 'tis to me? Would you prefer to me some straight-faced Puritan such as Sir Thomas Pugh be, he who heaps up gold and is content to give it to orphanages and goes to church twice on Sunday. Should you love me then the more were I such? Hardly, I should think," he continued without waiting her response. "You are the quintessential woman. You balk when you would raise my bile about my fault as a husband—my sickness you would sometimes put it—but you thrive on it as much as do I. I have done nothing in which you have not had a share, enjoying it more than I, should the truth be known.''

'' 'Tis a wife's duty to obey her husband,'' she said flatly, shrinking from his touch.

"But you sang another tune on our wedding night when you quenched my passion with your girlish timidity, praying that you might preserve your virginity still but a night or twain and begging me not to do you so roughly. Where was your wifely obedience then?''

She turned on him suddenly, her face aflame. "It was perhaps where your manhood was, for when you came to your own duty as husband you could not, but simpered like a child.''

His expression turned stony, the thin smile he wore continuously disappearing into lips pressed white with rage.

"Whore that you are,'' he bellowed, "you unmanned me. If I have done the devil's work since, it was you that drove me to it, depriving me of all pleasure but what I could have by looking on.''

He grabbed her by the throat viciously and threw her to the bed, yelping with pain as one of her knees found its way to his groin. His hands lost their grip, and she took that opportunity to gasp deeply for breath. His body lay heavily upon her, suffocating her, a great blanket of flesh defiling her. She dug her nails into his face once, then twice, and then felt drops of blood fall onto her breast as the pain drove him away from her. Both lay side by side breathing heavily, nursing their wounds, wishing the other dead.

"You would like to see me in my grave, wouldn't you?'' she said bitterly, her voice heavy with hatred. "But you have not what it takes to murder me yourself, although you are soon enough to find hirelings.''

"You disgust me,'' he said weakly, caressing his torn face. "As though I had found some monstrous animal in the barn, neither male nor female, fish nor fowl, but made of many parts, each horrible to look upon.''

"You may find me as you like. Other men know where, and how, to find me a woman.'' With that she rose quickly from the bed and went to her mirror to examine the reddening of her neck where he had tried to strangle her.

She said, "I thought myself one rich in fortune to come to a knight's bed his lawful wife. Now I see that the knight is merely a man, conniving, weak, and petty in his pleasures. You have won me to your will. I have played your curious games that would have made a sailor blush. And if I have enjoyed the game myself, I at least did not invent it. When I came to your bed I was a virgin. 'Tis true I lost my maidenhead painfully, for I was but sixteen and knew nothing of men or their ways. You could have been patient, gentle, understanding that. You were not so much older than I that you should not have given me a day or two to make the act natural and pleasant to me. If I can give myself to other men now with pleasure it is only because of such practice provided by you, and the pleasure and envy you have in looking on is a woman's way of revenge."

"Aye," he said. "That and refusing to bear me children."

She turned to him again, for the first time since their struggle. "Yes, a woman's revenge is that. I shall give you no pleasure of my body save that which you can get from seeing others enjoy it, and no child either."

He rose from the bed, his groin aching still with the pain of her kick, and came to where she stood by the mirror.

"We are more alike than you think," he said almost tenderly. "Perhaps that is why our hatred for one another is so enduring. We depend upon each other too much. Without me you would be nothing, for although you are fair you are poor and would be lucky to find another husband suited to your tastes."

"And why is it that you need me, other than for your toys?"

"I need you because we are not merely playmates but fellow conspirators. We are such that batten upon mutual distrust, perhaps because we dislike so much something within ourselves. Our hatred for one another gives a preferable vent to it."

"You are ever philosophical after a quarrel."

"You inspire many moods in me," he said with ill-concealed sarcasm.

Recognizing his change in tone, she turned and looked at him again. He stood there, his suit fitting him loosely as it did men large of frame, his black hair tousled, his thick lips formed into a kind of smile. She recognized the expression and, after the three years they had lived together, the significance of his carriage as he began walking toward her.

"We have quarreled and hurt one another," he said softly.

"It is but nine of the morning," she said, feeling his hands firmly on her shoulders.

"I have caused you pain," he said gently.

"You have caused me grievous pain in body and mind."

"I cannot undo now the pain I have caused in mind, yet I can ease the body."

"By yourself?" she asked, looking into his eyes curiously.

"May I not try?"

She suffered him to remove her gown. His hands were white and cold, and she shivered. Then he lifted her in his arms, carried her to the bed, and began undressing himself. She turned her face to the wall and waited until she felt the bed groan under his weight. He shut her eyes with his lips when he pulled her to him; she felt him kiss her neck. Then she resigned herself dutifully. She hardly felt him enter her; she was attentive only to his dead weight and heavy breathing, his effort to complete the act, and his ultimate failure. She thought, Is it because I do not love him, cannot love him? Then she began to giggle, softly at first, until her laughter became the howl of a wounded animal.

It was dark inside. In the corner Varnell saw Simon the hostler lying beneath blankets shivering. As he drew close, he could see that the man was caught in the grip of fever. He shook uncontrollably and his wrinkled face was flushed as though he had been bending over a fire.

Varnell knelt by the hostler, pushing aside the gray hairs

that had fallen down over his face. The hostler breathed heavily. "You are sick, man?" Varnell asked.

"Do I look well?" Simon croaked, his voice seeming to come not from his throat but from some subterranean region of his chest.

"I came down with the fever not two hours since, when I finished slopping the hogs. 'Twas the work the girl used to do before she drowned in the pond. Maybe 'tis a sign I will be the next to go, though they'll not be getting me to the water. I'll die in the straw, and let the rats pick my bones like they done the players' boy." Between wheezes, the man began to blubber.

My God, the secretary thought, the man's delirious. Suddenly he realized that should Simon die he would have confessed to a crime without a witness to testify to his limited part in it.

"Are you thirsty?" he asked urgently.

The hostler raised a hand, pointing to a pail in the corner of the stall. Varnell took the dipper, filled it full of the rank, cloudy liquid, and raised it to the hostler's lips. Simon's eyes remained glassy, as though caught up in some private vision.

"Does the innkeeper know that you are ill?"

Simon shook his head. Varnell gathered some straw to pillow the old man's head and hurried from the stable to the inn, where he found Master Rowley at his accounts. The innkeeper looked up sullenly from his work, obviously unhappy at the interruption.

"Did you know that your man Simon lies of the fever in the stable?"

The innkeeper scowled, gnawing at his lower lip. "What's that to me," he snarled. "Simon does little enough of his work when he is fit."

"But he may die," Varnell protested.

"If he does, I may find five boys in Chelmsford who will oblige me with their service at half his pay and earn their keep as he does not."

The secretary's heart sank. The man was obviously in a black mood and would not easily be moved to charity or pity, not on such a day as this.

"But he is your servant, shiftless or not, and you are bound by law to see to him," Varnell began, trying another tack.

The man placed his quill on the table beside him and rose to his full height. He spoke harshly. "And has the enforcing of laws been added to your duties, Master Secretary, that you come to trouble an honest man with your scurvy face?"

Varnell had, he well knew, no talent for physical adventures of the sort the innkeeper's wrath promised. He backed toward the door, his heart beating like a soldier's drum.

"Then I will see to the man myself," he said weakly as he pushed open the door and once again felt the drizzle of rain splash upon his bare head. The damp air and excitement of his encounter with the innkeeper had inspired him with a powerful need to move his bowels, but he made his way directly again to the stable to see to the hostler.

The man was clearly worse. His withered face now seemed bloated and purple. It crossed Varnell's mind that this illness might be no simple fever but the plague, and he shuddered fearfully. Yet he could not leave the man's side, for his witness to murder was not more essential than ever if he was to regain credit with his mistress.

Finally he could hold himself no longer, despite his anxiety about the hostler. He decided against making his way in the mud to the jakes and went instead into a darker corner of the stable and relieved himself. The release gave him pleasure, a little consolation in the midst of his discontent. When he returned, he found Simon even more incoherent, mumbling all manner of nonsense about demons and witches. Varnell removed a handkerchief from his pocket and mopped the man's brow. Simon's uncontrollable quivering and shaking now increased, and then suddenly he lay quiet. The hostler shut his eyes and began to breathe more softly.

Exhausted from the excitement, Varnell rested his head on his knees and soon after fell into a fitful sleep himself. He dreamed of his mistress again, as he had many nights of late. But in his restless slumber she appeared to him only in the vaguest of outlines, the familiar features of her face confused with those of his London whore. She drew toward him, her slender arms outstretched as though to embrace him lovingly. Then a look of horror fell upon her countenance as though she had just caught sight of some loathsome unnatural thing. The image vanished, then reappeared, but this time the face was that of the players' boy, his mouth agape in an agonizing voiceless scream. Varnell tried to scream too, but he could make nó sound. In his sleep he could feel the sweat running from his hair onto his nose and down the sides of his mouth. It ran into the thin hairs of his mustache.

He awoke abruptly, his heart racing and his legs painfully cramped. At once he looked to the hostler. The man's face was contorted. The eyes were open, staring at him vacantly, as though his last thought were some question, now quite irrelevant. Then Varnell saw the great rat sitting on the hostler's belly, his small black nose twitching nervously. He kicked out at the rat, awkwardly and ineffectually, emitting at the same time a cry of anger and disgust. The creature gave him a scornful look, then scampered into the recesses of the stable.

She daubed more powder on her neck, but just enough to hide the bruise his fingers had made. In the mirror she could see him waiting patiently for her to complete her dressing. She knew that he enjoyed watching all the little details of her toilet, the brushing of her hair, the application of powder and rouge and the perfumes, the adjusting of her braces and stays. She lingered at the task—not to please him, but to prolong her amusement at his fascination.

"You expect to get the girl back, then?" she asked casually.

"If I know my constable, he will be as good as his word. Varnell says he has arrested the twain for breaking of the peace. His next step is to bring both to me for judgment. I expect them all this hour."

Since she could not resist vexing him, she said, "My dear husband, you always have such confidence in your minions. Do you never think to be surprised one day when someone in your hire decides to follow his own inclination and not your own?''

''The day may come,'' he said curtly, obviously irritated at her effort to begin another quarrel. ''But I wait it very much as I expect the final judgment, with considerable disinterest.''

''Now I am ready,'' she said.

She took his arm, and he led her into his own chamber. From the window he could see that although the rain had stopped the sun had yet to dispell the pervasive gloom. The truth was that he himself was concerned that the constable was late in bringing the Welsh girl and the player to him, and his vexation was growing, though he was bound not to disclose it to his wife.

She, for her part, sat in his own favorite chair. ''You have plans should the constable not bring the girl?''

''How so?'' he said.

''Well, she has seen more than her share of what transpires in this house. It would hardly do to have her running about the country with stories. Those of her birth readily turn the plain truth to an elaborate scandal to the discredit of their betters, but she has a simple plain tale that would burn the ears of every butter-and-egg burgher of the town where it to get out. And she seems to have become fond of this player whom Richard Mull knew well.''

''If Master Stock has not shown his dull countenance at the door by noon, I shall proceed to his shop and root the wench from whichever closet he has concealed her in.''

''Ah,'' she said, her eyes agleam with mockery, ''to say such of him in whom you had put such confidence.''

Her husband said nothing. She rose and walked to the window, lost in her thoughts. The secretary had been right, of course, although by instinct her dissembled disbelief fit the circumstances. Her husband had had the boy killed. The exact motive was not important to her. She had been fond of Richard, had found in his ardor the beginnings of real desire, and yet she could not regret his death, however she tried. And whatever horror she might have one time felt for the blood upon her husband's hands was now lost in her general contempt for him. Satisfying his curious whims was her method of control, the only method for a woman in her position, without friends or relatives and, worse, without financial resources of her own to sustain her.

She had not seen Master Varnell that day, although he had been eager enough to do her bidding on the previous evening when he promised to bring the hostler to her. She detested the man with his social pretensions and clammy hands. And yet she knew that he could do her service, that he waited in line as had others for some sign of encouragement, for some promise of more intimate reward than money. Well, she would give signs and promise subtly and give her body too if the occasion required, but she would give them no satisfaction that used her, that was sure.

The rain had stopped. He was hungry, tired, and drenched to the bone. Worst of all, he felt completely ruined. He had risked all in hope of favor, and now all that he could contemplate was at best dismissal from his master's service, at worst the gibbet. He rode on slowly, trying to avoid the great accumulation of water. He could not rid his mind of the bloated face of the hostler, the blank, questioning eyes, still moist with life.

He stabled the horses and walked slowly and deliberately to the Hall, entering his chamber through the kitchen, careful to avoid the cooks who were already preparing dinner. In his room he took off his cloak and hat, his drenched doublet, and shivered awhile half-naked while he searched through his chest for something to dry himself with. Then he dressed in a fresh suit, used the chamber pot, and powdered his face. Confronting his mistress was unavoidable. He wondered whether she would believe this new turn of events, or whether she would think his news of the hostler's death a stratagem to avoid bringing the man to her. He took a deep breath, deciding to make the best of his ill-luck.

While on his way, he was informed by another household servant that Cecilia Saltmarsh was in her husband's chamber, information he took as a sign of fortune, since it permitted him to postpone their interview. Then feeling hungry, he descended to the buttery in hope of finding some leftovers from last night's supper.

In the larder he found a piece of beef, a small cheese, and two leeks, from which he made a simple but satisfying meal. Full of stomach, he somehow felt more secure; perhaps, after all, he might find his mistress in a credulous disposition, in which case his story might stand even in the absence of the hostler's corroboration. From the small pantry window, he saw that the sun had finally emerged from the clouds, and this too began to brighten his mood. Of the horrible events in the stable he tried not to think.

He decided to walk in the desolate garden, since he had no more copying to do and his mind was too preoccupied with the business at hand in any case. He had taken but two turns when he saw Lady Saltmarsh emerge from the house and walk toward him. His heart leaped with anticipation.

"You are enjoying the sun, Master Secretary?" she said graciously.

"I do, lady," he replied, encouraged by her greeting.

She whispered, although they had the garden to themselves, "You have brought me the hostler?"

He paused and then replied, "Alas, lady, he is dead, of the fever. I found him so early this morning when I went to the inn to fetch him hither."

He withdrew the five coins she had given him from his pocket and handed them to her. "Since I could not therefore accomplish my task, I return my share to you as well."

She looked at him in what he interpreted as a friendly manner and he felt relieved of spirit.

"Well," she said, "perhaps God's justice has been done on the instrument of my husband's vengeance. You see I believe you. A dream I had yesternight confirmed it. Do you believe that dreams reveal waking truths, Master Secretary?" she continued, taking his arm.

They strolled near where an ornamental well was festooned with plaster nymphs and satyrs. He followed at her side obediently, choked with happiness.

"I owe you an apology, I am afraid. Your story at first caused me great grief, for my husband as well as young

Richard Mull. Perhaps I should then have told you the truth but knew not if I could repose complete confidence in you.''

He began to protest, but she stayed him with her hand and proceeded: ''The truth is that Richard Mull, although a charming boy and proficient actor, misunderstood my interest in him and took advantage of it. Not that he meant me any disrespect, I am sure, or that he behaved unseemly toward me, but my husband is a very jealous man. He must be forgiven if in his rage he gave such orders that in a more reasonable temper he would have scorned to contemplate.''

''Well, yes,'' Peter Varnell began, trying to apply this new interpretation to what he recalled of the interview in which his employer had paid him ten crowns to hire the hostler to do the murder.

But she stayed his response again, taking him by the arm again and leading him to where a miniature grove of trees marked the end of the garden and the beginning of the fields. When they were in the grove and concealed from the view of the house, she said, ''Now I am afraid you must do something else for me, if it be in your power.''

''Oh, I would do anything, lady.''

''I shall not ask you to do anything,'' she continued playfully, ''but rather something in particular, which if you satisfy me in this will make it a profit to you in more ways than one. The constable delays in bringing my serving girl to my husband. Every moment we delay in this she has more opportunity to blacken my husband's reputation in the town. I fear now that she hath told her tale to the constable and his wife and to the player and God knows who else. Deny her tales should they be credited. Give the girl's character. You might mention, although this was privy between me and her, that I had found her in my private cabinet, had charged her with theft, which she to me readily confessed, and for such I dismissed her the day she left—and that this, then, is the ground of her talebearing. It will seem all the more probable, her running away, and with a player. Moreover, you may say that I had it from more than one manservant that she freely admitted them to her chamber, where they did their will with her.''

"If this be so, lady, 'twere best to have the men themselves swear to it.''

She paused, as though reflecting on his advice. "Such witnesses are indeed always best, and yet methinks that one of your learning will make a better testimony if such should be the need.''

"I understand perfectly, lady. You may depend on me.''

"I know I may," she responded, extending her hand to his so that a thrill of delight ran from his wrist to his groin and warmed him.

"As for now," she continued, "you must mind my husband's business, but be prepared as need to be defend our honors with your words to them in the town who are always ready to lend an ear to such scandals.

" 'Tis only too true,'' Varnell agreed sympathetically as mistress and servant made their way from the grove to the gravel walk and back to the Hall.

"Let us too," she said, "keep this conversation privily between us. There is no need to cause my husband concern, who is already tormented that I should suffer humiliation from a servant's lies. I have tried to convince him, perhaps not with great success, that I discount such mendacity and would not have him discover that I have had to be so bold in enlisting your support of us.''

Again she extended her hand and he bent low to kiss it. Then she smiled softly and went into the house through the great hall.

Varnell went directly to his chamber. He flung off his boots, threw himself on his bed, and began to reflect with growing delight on the day's events. She had believed his account after all, even providing him a justification and forgiveness for his own complicity in the murder, a thing she would hardly have done, he reasoned, did she not feel genuine affection for him. How empty are these fears and omens to which fond men give credence, he thought; how quickly fortune spins her wheel and turns catastrophe to triumph. He almost laughed for joy, but then he began to regret the two hours he had spent beside the dying hostler and determined to find the handkerchief with which he had mopped the man's feverish brow and burn it forthwith.

11

AT DAWN they breakfasted on eggs and cheese, bid Big Tod and Gwen Godspeed on their journey to London, and Joan turned her thoughts to the day's business in the shop while her husband called to Philip to saddle the horse, for he would ride to the Hall, the road being too muddy to endure by foot or trust to the cart.

He had slept fitfully, awakening once from a dream of vague but disturbing shapes to mutter a prayer and crawl closer to Joan, breathing softly next to him. He felt tired, as though he had not slept at all.

"What will you say to him?" she had asked when they were alone, not bothering to explain to whom she had referred.

"I will say the truth, that I am permitted by law to free at my own discretion those charged with breaking of the peace and that in this instance I took advantage of the privilege."

"I fear he will take it badly."

"Aye, he may, but in any case I have done what I have done."

To that she said nothing, but went about her duties, calling Alice and Betty to the cleaning above and the apprentice boy to open the shop to early custom.

Matthew rode slowly, once mounted, for the street would not bear a gallop, this being market day and the town full of countryfolk loaded with wares. Besides he was in no hurry, for as he contemplated another interview with the magistrate he found his new knowledge of the man's private life more a burden than a help. He felt tainted by his knowledge, his innocence lost. Joan had been right all along.

At the Hall he was admitted at once, an efficiency that only added to his apprehension. He had not decided just how he was to explain himself to Saltmarsh. It was within his power, he knew, to let the actor and the maid go free, but he feared his freeing of them injudicious. He had tried to read the old servingman's face, to find in the man's eyes or set of lips some forewarning of the wrath to come, but he might have been the curate making the parish rounds for all Daniel's face revealed of his master's state of mind.

"You are up early; that's good," Saltmarsh said, advancing to meet him. "You have brought my wife's girl and the player?"

"I released them this morning, satisfied that they would cause no disturbance, and they are by now five miles for London."

He had told the truth outright, not stopping once he had begun but letting it all out so that the full measure of the magistrate's response might be obtained with equal promptness. He did not wish to prolong the unpleasantness of the scene.

Saltmarsh scowled with displeasure. "I see," he said. "You took it upon yourself to do this?"

"Sir, I saw it within my charge. My cellar is but small. 'Twill hold few malefactors, and this being market day, I thought it better to let them be who had done no more than occasion a quarrel. There was no harm done."

Saltmarsh walked to the window to gaze on some distant object. "Did not my secretary inform you that the girl was a runaway from my service and that it was for this reason I wished her returned forthwith?"

"He did, sir, and charged her as bound to you. Yet he provided no proof, and such would be required in a court of law before the girl might be held."

Saltmarsh turned abruptly. "Was not my secretary's word proof enough. Need I have come myself? And if I had done, would you have been so bold as to call me a liar."

Matthew began a reply, but the magistrate's next outburst prevented it. "You may take your leave, Master Stock, both of this house and of your office. I will keep no servant I cannot rule, nor constable either. You have stood between me and my will. I will not tolerate it."

Saltmarsh was screaming with rage; his eyes blazed and saliva formed little bubbles in the corners of his mouth. Matthew stepped backward in alarm, ready if needful to ward off a blow. He had been prepared for anger, but anger of the sort he was accustomed to in persons of authority—cold, calculated, and restrained. There was something patently absurd in the magistrate's raving, and yet Matthew felt the firm grip of fear. The man was mad, really mad.

"I beg your forgiveness if I have offended—"

"If you have offended? If you have offended?"

"Sir, I—"

"Get out! Be off!"

Matthew turned on his heels, not waiting for the servingman to show him the way out.

Saltmarsh cursed God, long and vilely. He hated to be crossed, and he had been so served by everyone within his house—the Welsh girl, his wife, and now the constable. He felt as though he must thrash out at something; he would have destroyed some of the chamber's furnishings had he not remembered the cost. But it had no sooner come upon him that his fit began to subside. His head ceased to pound, his chest to heave; he paced the floor nervously contemplating his next move. He remembered the priest—a fool but one who could be of use. Fear would make him pliant enough, and if not fear then the man's lust would put the priest in his pocket. Saltmarsh felt better at the thought; he felt the master again.

When the priest entered several hours later, Saltmarsh sat composed and dignified, but he immediately observed in the man's manner a strange confidence of step and expression. He bid Saltmarsh good day as though the two had just met upon the road, accepted without hesitation a comfortable chair, and sat, his legs crossed, his eyes clear and guileless. Saltmarsh decided to remain standing, if only to have the advantage in height and bulk. So the man had found his backbone. That would make the game all the more to his liking, and the victory to his credit, he reflected.

Saltmarsh began: "I have determined, to my regret, that I may have been overhasty in accepting my wife's account of the incident. Women often misconstrue a word, a glance of the eye. A man may fall into sin and be up to his neck before he knows it."

Saltmarsh watched surprise betrayed on the priest's features with dumb amusement. It was an ill mariner who could not catch the wind from some direction. He continued: "You are a priest, though in your violation of my wife you have acted wrongly, for which I pray God forgive you. Yet you have some knowledge from your calling of the nature of women?"

"Some knowledge, perhaps," the priest replied uncertainly.

"Well, then you must know that although 'tis the nature of women to submit to their husbands, there be some who are so reluctant to do so that canon law disjoins them."

"You speak of conjugal relations?"

"I do."

The priest's voice had been steady at first; now a quivering betrayed his puzzlement. "But," he said, "I do not see how this pertains, for if you will pardon my recalling it, your wife seems a proper woman in all respects."

"Aye, and so she may be with some men, but unfortunately she is not with her lawful husband."

"I see," the priest said, obviously puzzled still.

"Ah," Saltmarsh said wistfully, "I wonder if you do." He clasped his hands behind his back and walked toward the window, where he stood staring for some time while the priest sat in silence, feeding, Saltmarsh felt sure, on his curiosity. When he believed sufficient time to have passed, he proceeded, but if anything, with even more circumspection.

"We are both men of understanding, of experience. Although 'tis my shame to admit it, my wife does not follow natural courses, but prefers her pleasure from strange men. You are not the first in whose arms I have found her, and perhaps that is why I am now so ready to forgive you. You see I have had practice—in forgiving. 'Tis a godly thing to do, is it not?"

"Most assuredly, sir."

"Well, then, you see that I do have my virtues, do I not?"

"Most certainly."

"Then I must tell you that I too have my foibles, one of which being that although I detest my wife's unnatural affection I suffer it, for her sake, for I love her more than my life and would sooner give her pleasure, though indirectly, than see her want."

Saltmarsh turned suddenly to note the effect of this on the priest and was pleased to find him off guard still, for he sat in his chair as a schoolboy browbeaten by a stern master.

"You are indeed a most tolerant husband," the priest said with genuine amazement.

"Let us say 'forgiving.' The word is more apt, is it not?"

The priest agreed, then said, "But I understand not yet how I might rectify my abuse of you, sir. For indeed you were my host, and I did sin against you as well as God."

Saltmarsh paused, reflecting on the question as though it were at that very moment that the precise way to the priest's redemption was to be determined. "You may," he proceeded, "do two things. First, resolve me in my mind whether my forgiveness in such a case be allowable before God."

"Sir, although I be before the bench myself in this affair, I can honestly say that no man would blame you were your

138

sword to find its home in my breast, but also that the angels will praise you with the saints were you to be forgiving.''

Saltmarsh smiled and approached him genially. "Then might you resolve me also in this, as to whether my forgiveness of my wife's fault might lawfully be extended to facilitate it, to the end that her natural wants be not denied.''

The priest paused, then said, " 'Tis a difficult question, out of my ken who am not versed in the thornier issues of casuistry. And yet I should think that were one to be sanctioned, the allowance of the other would follow hard upon.''

"Good," Saltmarsh replied goodheartedly. "Then might the satisfaction of my wife be the work of a sound man, or to put it in another way, would the lover's act be sanctioned in such a case?''

The priest hesitated again, avoiding Saltmarsh's eyes. " 'Twould be adultery, plain and simple,'' he replied haltingly.

"And yet is there not a higher law, one that in such an extraordinary case as this might—''

"I think not, Sir Henry. Adultery 'twould be.''

"But consider this, man,'' Saltmarsh began earnestly. "Does it not follow that if an act be to a good end, then the act itself be good and the actor justified?''

The priest let this settle, prying his eyes from the floor to meet those of the man before him. "You have matched me in logic, sir. I grant you that the doer of a good act is justified in any case.''

"Then," Saltmarsh concluded triumphantly, "would it run against your profession to continue to serve my wife and me in this? For I know you now to be no common lecher but a gentleman bred, fallen from grace not by your own will but by the power of my wife's beauty.''

"Do you intend me for your wife's lover, then?'' the priest asked, with astonishment.

"I do, for I tell you that I have no greater desire in this life than that every desire of hers be fulfilled. If she has chosen you among others, then I shall choose you as well and give you my hand upon it.''

Saltmarsh extended his hand to the priest, who sat still yet, as though he had awakened from a deep sleep to find himself at court without his boots. After a moment or two he rose and allowed himself to be led to the door. As they passed into the great hall, Saltmarsh whispered, "Master Hayforth, there is one thing yet that I would ask of you concerning your new duties in the house. 'Tis a special favor that might make you feel . . . awkward . . . at first, but you will get accustomed to it and it will give me no little satisfaction."

As he left Saltmarsh's chamber, the priest felt emotionally depleted and confused. He had expected another angry confrontation with an outraged husband, more threats of violence and imprisonment, and a hailstorm of curses. In their place he had found a most willing cuckold, a hypocritical villain, and a logic chopper who was quicker to rectify an infamous appetite than a dozen fanatical Puritans their gluttony. And like a kindly old uncle, the man had led him from his private chamber with the most outrageous invitation yet. The priest thought himself well traveled in the realms of lust, but he had never seen the like.

Though bizarre, the arrangement would have piqued his interest had his amorous encounter with Cecilia Saltmarsh not left such a bad taste in his mouth. If only the woman he had thought her to be had graced his sheets rather than the cold and calculating whore who, if her husband's tale was to be credited, was more wonderful in her appetite than in her frigidity.

Well, he concluded, Cecilia Saltmarsh should howl for a week before he would do her service, in bed or otherwise. At that he went quickly to his chamber and secured the door from within. For a long time he sat on his bed thinking. Then he quickly gathered his few things and made his way as quietly from the house as he could, using the escape route Cecilia Saltmarsh had shown him on the day of his arrival.

There was no time to secure another mount in town. He walked toward the lodge and then to the highway where he hoped to hail the London coach, although he had no idea of its schedule. The road was empty of traffic and nearly dry except in those places where wagons and coaches had left ruts. These he avoided carefully, keeping his eyes fixed to the road, occasionally turning to look behind him, half fearing to see Saltmarsh or one of his toadies in pursuit. But the Hall sat as forlorn as Babylon. Only a thin curl of smoke making its way heavenward from one of the chimneys betrayed the life within. Then he reached the brow of the hill and the great house disappeared from sight.

He had no sooner become conscious of the stillness, the unnerving desolation of the fields and woods, but it was broken by the distant rhythm of horses' feet. To his view the road to the north remained empty still. Then from over the hill he saw the top of a coach, and then the coach itself bearing down upon him. He halted in his way, stepping to the side of the roadway and lifting an arm for a signal. When the driver made no effort to slow the team, the priest stepped to the center of the road and began to wave both hands, thinking perhaps the driver thought him but a gawking country man. But the coach came on, if anything increasing its speed, and by the time the priest recognized the driver as the ill-faced groom from the Hall it was too late to leap from danger. He did not have time to cry out in terror before he was caught between the first pair of horses and dragged beneath the coach.

At the same moment that the priest met his death on the London road, Matthew entered his shop pleased to find his wife and assistant Thomas beyond the counter seeing to the needs of a half dozen prosperous-looking customers. Joan gave him a quick glance and a smile, then proceeded with the business at hand. Well, he thought, his news might wait, being mixed of good and ill. He removed his hat and cloak, hung both on the rack by the door, and rolled up his sleeves ready to resume his familiar trade. But after a few minutes about his business, he realized that it was simply not the same. He would not for the world have remained constable still, but the unresolved murder of the players' boy remained a piece of unfinished business that he was hard put to ignore, private citizen or no.

Toward late afternoon the shop became empty as customers milled in the streets, feeding upon market-day dainties and the entertainment of minstrels attracted by the crowd.

"Well, that's that," Joan said philosophically when he had told her of his dismissal. "I hope it hasn't put you out of sorts."

"I am at once relieved and vexed," he replied thoughtfully. "And yet I know that had I never been elected constable in the first place I would never have missed the honor. Now that I think the better on it, maybe it is not the office but the particular commission. This whole week I have given to the resolution of a crime. Now that I am done with it I feel as though I had been deprived of a right."

She brought him porridge and a short pot of ale. "Well," she said after a few moments of thought, "the town know Saltmarsh and they know you, and if from that they take you as nought else but abused, I'll miss my guess."

"Ah, Joan," he said affectionately, "did honors depend upon your word, I would be knight."

She laughed and removed the few simple utensils. Of the porridge he had eaten little. "You may be knight yet, and not upon my word but on that of those hereabouts who know you for the good man you are."

He reached out to embrace her, but she danced away girlishly. "Will you flirt with me?" he said, laughing.

"Aye, I will," she replied coyly. " 'Tis a woman's way."

"In that case, let Thomas see to the afternoon's business, while you and I recall our youth."

She snorted with mock outrage. "Youth? Hardly need I recall what I've never lost, man. I know not about you."

"So you will play married to an old man, will you? Then I'll show you a thing." He bounded after her, just missing her apron strings as she darted behind a counter. Plump and well girded with stays and petticoats, she was nonetheless fleet of foot, and Matthew soon found himself breathless.

"You see how a simple woman can put you to work,"

she said, grinning slyly. "Agree to that in principle, and you shall have me as you will."

"A good man of business will never pass up such an offer. Besides I fear for our reputations should we be suddenly interrupted by someone thinking that this be a place of business and not of courting as we have now made it."

She led the way up to their chamber and he watched while she undressed, as unashamed as though she were alone; and yet at the same time her face bore both the confidence of love and the expectation of its pleasures. When she was in bed, lying in the afternoon sunlight streaming through the great bay window of their chamber, he removed his own clothing. Her eyes were shut but he knew she was not asleep.

Later they whispered, neither able to sleep but both too drowsy to rise.

"Saltmarsh is as guilty as sin," he said firmly. "Of that there's no more doubt than chickens have feathers. But he's a close man, mistrustful, and wonderfully subtle in his courses."

" 'Twould be a bad one to do business with, but he's a devil as magistrate, for 'tis he that needs the watching."

"Now that Big Tod and his girl have left town, we alone know of his dirty work."

"And yet," she reminded him, "we know very little of that, hardly the why of it and not the method at all—and none of it will endure proving. Were we to accuse him, he might charge us back with slander, especially now that your dismissal permits him to lay any of our charges to resentment."

"Aye, we have hardly ground upon to stand, and yet I am unwilling to let so great a devil have his will with us, and 'tis with us. He has abused us all, even though but one has died of it."

"Two," she reminded him. "The girl at the inn would be alive to this day had the boy not died."

"Who knows who else has met a bad end by his hands," he said in a hushed voice, as though the enormity of the crime forbade the utterance of it. "Unnatural courses such as his may well lead a man to any manner of act."

143

"And yet what may we do?" she asked earnestly.

The shop bell below prevented his reply. He sat up in the bed, feeling the chill of the air despite the sunshine on his bare chest.

"Thomas will see to it," she said.

"No, 'tis too long we have tarried now. I am a merchant, not a courtier who lies abed till noon and is most fond of love when the sun can bear witness to it."

She laughed. "You are both merchant and lover, my lover, and 'tis to your credit that you understand the mystery of mixing pleasure with business."

He pulled on his breeches and fastened his cotton jerkin. He felt under the bed for his boots and then, thinking the better of it, returned them to his closet for the more comfortable shoes he was used to wearing about the shop. He would not go from the shop that day on Saltmarsh's business or his own. Joan lay still under the covers.

"I'm to work," he said.

She sighed goodhumoredly. "Man—and woman—was cursed with it. Since there's no help, come let us work."

"And yet," he said, hesitating at the threshold of their bedchamber, "there must yet be some way of bringing Saltmarsh to justice. My knowledge of his doings lie so heavily upon me that I can do little else but scratch among the facts of the case."

She responded with surprising cynicism: "You may scratch long and hard, like Alice's hens of the yard, but since 'tis a gentleman's crime you seek to uncover you must not expect a ready hand from the law. That ground is hard."

"Greater than he have met their ends by the rule of law," he called over his shoulder, descending the stairs to the shop.

From his window, Saltmarsh watched the groom return with the coach, dismount, unharness the horses, and lead them to the stable. He watched still while the man began walking slowly toward the Hall, his face hard as usual, as though completely absorbed in the meditation of some private vice.

144

Saltmarsh waited for the knock at his chamber door. The groom had returned quickly, just as the knight had thought the whole thing out upon seeing the priest flee from the house. Saltmarsh cursed his luck to have found himself surrounded by such incompetence in so few number of days. The priest would have served his purposes nicely had abject fear or something else, Saltmarsh knew not what, not driven him off and created the new threat of the disclosure of his affairs. Evidently that threat was now past.

He admitted the groom, who on this occasion did not break his habitual silence.

"Is it done?" Saltmarsh asked simply, to which the man nodded and held out his hand for the payment.

Saltmarsh went to his desk and withdrew from a drawer a small coffer. From among the silver he picked what he thought the man's trouble was worth, reasoning that since the groom's regular duties involved driving of the coach a mishap on the road, at no risk to the driver, could hardly be worth much.

The groom looked into his open palm and seemed not so much to reckon the amount of the money as to savor the heft of it. Then he bowed sullenly and withdrew.

Saltmarsh had not asked about the details. And yet he regretted now that the priest was not available for service. Violence always made him itch in the groin, even when vicarious. In a day or so he would be back in London, where the satisfaction of his pleasures would be easy enough, but that was a day or two away.

There came a knocking at his door. It was the whey-faced secretary armed with letters and documents of various sorts.

"You have been busy this morning, Master Varnell?" Saltmarsh asked with polite curiosity.

"I have, sir, and am now done with four letters and as many contracts, which, if it pleases you to sign them, will bring my labors this day to an end."

"Indeed, and have you no more work?"

"No more to my knowledge."

In that case, then," Saltmarsh said, "I may find something else to occupy you during the afternoon."

Varnell looked up, his face contorted in a foolish grin, and placed the papers on the desk.

Saltmarsh sat down and, taking the letters one by one, quickly perused their contents and signed each with a bold flourish.

"I admire your hand, Master Varnell. 'Tis neat and tidy, and yet I think manly as well."

"Thank you, sir," the secretary replied, now all smiles. "I learned it at Cambridge from a tutor who had studied in Italy. There, he said, all the gentlemen practice it as an art."

"Well," Saltmarsh said, not bothering to look up, "you have learned it well enough."

Peter Varnell's smile broadened even more as he squirmed with delight at the compliment.

Saltmarsh shuffled the letters and contracts into a neat bundle and gave his secretary his instructions: "See that Master Philips has the contracts before supper, and while you are in town you may post the letters. With luck you will not have missed the last coach for London.

"Oh, Master Varnell," Saltmarsh called as the secretary was about to be off, "I may have more for you today. When therefore you return to the Hall I would appreciate it if you would wait upon me here. I would speak of the matter now but must consult my wife first. You won't forget?"

The secretary, pleased with the prospect of another confidence, assured his master that he would not forget, that he would conduct his business with dispatch, and return to the Hall before dark.

As soon as Peter Varnell had left, Saltmarsh went to his wife's chamber, where he found her supervising the packing of several large chests.

"I see you have begun your preparations early enough," he said agreeably, anxious to put things right with her.

His wife looked up, shrewdly gauging her husband's mood before responding. "You see truly," she responded. "I shall be less likely to forget what I am a long time considering."

Sensing that her husband's visit was prompted by more

than a desire to chat, with a gesture of the hand she dismissed the new maid. Then she stood, arms akimbo, waiting for him to divulge the reason for interrupting her labors.

"Your priest will not return," he began bluntly. "He has met with an accident on the highway." He hesitated, alert to her response, but she, catching the drift of his hesitation, put on a face of indifference, as though he had just reported a dead robin in the courtyard.

"Yet the church may thrive," she said when she had held him sufficiently in suspense. She began to gather a pile of petticoats to stuff in the largest of her chests.

"You are cold," he muttered, almost to himself.

She turned on him suddenly, dropping her voice to a growl. "And do you think I know not by whom the accident was brought to pass? There are no accidents in this house not of your making. Say I am cold? Yes, in truth I am so, but made so by you, who have no fear of God that you so violate his laws."

He parried to match the virulence of her reply. "Why, I'm damned if you don't sound like the vicar's wife, more concerned for his salvation than he himself. Who taught you morality that lecture me for murder? In all these things you have always proved a ready accomplice. 'Twas you who agreed to let him join us here, providing him with such entertainment—and I use the word with caution—as he imagined in his heart."

"Yes," she returned bitterly, her eyes filled with tears of rage, "but 'twas you, husband, who proposed it, and I may now ask you just why it was necessary to again dip our hands in blood."

He breathed heavily, beginning to pace so that his anger might subside. "Because, wife, he knew too much of our affairs."

"But did he not agree to stay on under the conditions you named? You told me thus yourself but only this morning. Will nothing please your fancy but you must humiliate me with these games of yours until I know not whom to give myself to nor why?"

"He so agreed," Saltmarsh responded more calmly, "but had no sooner done so but took flight from the house.

I saw him from the window, confirming what Daniel had told me earlier, that the priest was in his chamber packing with great haste. Daniel thought he might be carrying off the silver in his pack. To us he is a greater risk than the Welsh girl, whose mind to marriage may make what passed here stale in a month's time. But the priest, and thanks to your cold treatment of him, would be hot to report our doings to the first bishop he could catch by the coattails, Roman or no.''

"My cold treatment of him!" she protested wildly. "And were you also beyond the arras on that occasion that you so misjudge me?''

"I judge you by solid inference. Had he found you to his liking, or you to his, he would have stayed, for that man's priesthood is a thin stream to the river of his lust. I know such when I see 'em, reading it in their eyes.''

She sat down on her bed, arms hung between her legs, her golden hair loose about her bare shoulders. He had defeated her, he thought, at least for the moment. His sense of victory invited mercy, so he approached her slowly and deliberately and joined her on the bed.

"I have only done what must be done to protect the both of us" he said. "By this time tomorrow we shall be well on our way to London, and if we return here in less than six month's time 'twill be because the town has burned or the plague come again. I promise you that.''

"Will there be no public outcry at the man's death?" she asked weakly.

"He was a stranger. He knew no one in the town, save for those he met here, and they seemed to take little interest in him. To my knowledge, the body has not been found, and may not be; and when it will be found, who can say it was else that killed but the London coach, not ours. If the body is ever found. Thickets abound along the road.''

"Still I like not the idea of killing a priest.''

"Even such a one as he?''

"He was a priest," she said.

"Well, let them all die, for me," he said with disgust. "I never knew one of the cloth that was no less hypocritical than the Puritan sort. All words to candy o'er their appetite.''

She sat silently, as though her energy was spent, and Saltmarsh suddenly realized that although her sharp tongue was often hard to bear her silence was a weapon as well, and one that he might feel more painfully. He groped for something to pull her from her melancholy but could think of nothing. He was about to broach the topic of the secretary, who while he regarded the man with no little contempt yet he was a man who had cast fond glances at his mistress and breathed hotly in her presence. But it would not do to bring up that possibility now, even though the scene it conjured up in his imagination had the virtue of being bizarre, the man was such a pallid, effeminate creature. Saltmarsh turned to go, but she prevented it with a final word, softly but deliberately phrased.

"See to it, Harry, that there be no more deaths in this house or hereabouts. If there be, you may find yourself in want of a wife, for each day poverty without you seems more appealing than wealth with you.''

"You say that in the midst of plenty," he said sharply and turned to go, relishing the irony of his words.

12

" 'T IS CHADWICK the carrier."

"What? This early?"

"He says they have found a dead man by the road, a gentleman. He wishes you to come and see it. They've brought the body up in Chadwick's cart." Joan had that morning been long dressed before him, supervising the baking in the kitchen below. Now her face was heavy with concern.

"I told them you were no longer constable—which they had not heard but insist that there be no other yet appointed. You, it seems, must do for them."

Matthew fastened the last button of his coat and brushed his coal black hair straight back from his forehead. Joan followed him down the stairs into the shop, where Chadwick waited with several other men of the town whose names and faces Matthew knew well.

" 'Tis another dead 'un, Matthew." Tall, angular Spencer Beam leaned upon one of the counters surveying the little clothier with his narrow face screwed up in a frown. The other men, Will Freeman and Cyriac Smythe, looked on solemnly.

"I would 'ave missed 'im most entire had not Joty

missed 'er footin' and near stumbled by the way. There 'twas, only his white hands sticking from 'neath the thicket. Like claws. When I lifted im, I knew in a minute 'twas dead as stone, so heavy 'twas.''

While the carrier was completing his account, Matthew nodded a greeting to the men. He called Philip to fetch the lantern and then led the group into the street. It was dawning in the east.

They had thrown a blanket over the body, but from its frayed edges hands and feet protruded. Matthew shuddered and lifted the blanket to look at the man's face. By lantern the priest seemed younger than Matthew had remembered.

Joan had quietly stolen up behind him to peer over his shoulder. ''Why 'tis the priest,'' she gasped.

''Priest or no,'' muttered Spencer Beam, ''the man has met an ugly death. Doubtless the London coach caught him in a fog. It looks as if he were drug a ways.''

Mutely they watched the still corpse, as though expecting any moment that the priest would come alive to report on his own mishap. Matthew reached over to shut the eyes, but they would not shut. He pulled the blanket back over the face.

''As my wife has said''—Matthew began looking about him into the sober faces of the townsmen—''I am no longer constable of this parish. Word of this must go to the Hall. I cannot think it but mischance, and would so report it myself.''

''I wonder that the coach did not stop. The priest is no small man. He would have made a noise when the coach hit. Surely no blame would have fallen upon the coachman for what was never his fault.''

At this the men turned to look at Joan, as though they expected her now to put into words the vague uneasiness they all felt. Made bold by her perception of their uncertainties, she proceeded: ''Had the night been that dark, I should think the coach would have traveled slowly and thereby seen the poor man. Besides, if I remember right, yesternight the moon was full and the sky cloudless.''

''Why right she be,'' Cyriac Symthe affirmed in a thin

voice. "I saw clearly, and the wind did not suffer clouds, not as I recall."

"But 'tis certain," a deeper voice began, "that the man's been hit and drug, or one would think 'twere highwaymen. See if he has his purse about him."

Matthew pulled back the tattered blanket and found the priest's purse attached securely to his belt.

"The purse is safe," he informed them. " 'Twas not robbery that did this. And now I am of my wife's mind that 'twas no accident either."

"Will you look into the matter, Matthew, or should we proceed direct to the magistrate?"

Matthew did not respond to Spencer Beam's question at once, simple though it was, for it was his question as well. That he had no authority now to act officially for the parish was sure, and yet he wrestled still with a vague sense of obligation. Besides, this new death had pricked his curiosity. That it had some connection with the death of the players' boy he had no doubt.

"I will proceed to Sir Henry with this," he decided even as the words tripped from his mouth. "The priest's been brought to my own door and 'tis true I have as much interest in the parish as the next man."

"Or woman," Joan said behind him. "In faith, we have had more deaths of unnatural causes this one week than in my recollection."

The men murmured their agreement and, satisfied that the matter was now in capable hands, bid farewell to the clothier and his wife and went about their business.

"Bear the body to the curate," Matthew instructed the carrier. "The man had no relations in these parts. 'Tis the parish must pay for his burial."

"Will you have breakfast before going to the Hall?" Joan asked.

"Aye, I will, for what I am about to say to Sir Henry in this new matter has yet to come upon me. It may do so while I eat."

The aroma of bread drew them into the kitchen, where Alice had furnished the sturdy oak table with bowls of hot porridge, cheese, and mugs of ale. Husband and wife took their usual places, Matthew said grace, and both began to eat in silence.

Then Joan said, "I wonder what might the priest have done to bring him to this end?"

Her husband shrugged and cut himself a large share of the soft cheese. "I thought once that the ways of those who take others' lives were as simple to be known as why a man should wish to eat, or heap up gold, or go to heaven when he died. Now I understand less."

She contemplated this remark between swallows of porridge. Then she reasoned, "If Sir Henry's hand has done this, you will have little from him beyond a curse for your persistence."

"Indeed," he responded flatly, finishing his cheese and beginning in earnest on his mug of ale. "Yet will I speak with him and be damned, for though I be constable no more, yet I am a townsman with a townsman's rights."

"But now you have no office, no authority," she protested, glad for his determination but fearful of where it might lead him.

"True. Yet will I speak with him nonetheless, for I be as sure the priest's death was conceived at the Hall as the death of the players' boy."

Joan herself was no less curious as to the cause of the priest's death, and no less certain of its place of conception. And yet in the last few days she had found herself nearly overwhelmed with a sense of futility. There was, she now accepted, no evidence for what she knew intuitively, and no safe way to bring the evildoer to justice even were there evidence to substantiate her intuition. She ceased eating to marvel at her husband's appetite, especially in light of what he was about to undertake. She realized suddenly that the unyielding pursuit of a goal which she had sometimes found mere willfulness now showed itself as courage. As for her husband, he was not so much mindful of his virtues as excited by the prospect of his next confrontation with the magistrate.

After gulping the last of his ale, Matthew stuffed a piece of cheese in his pocket, brushed his wife's face with half a kiss, and seized his cloak like a man who had just heard where he might find pounds for shillings. In the street he walked briskly, nodding now and again at a passerby, customer, or friend, his mind already at work on the words and phrases with which he would present these new circumstances to Saltmarsh. They did not come easily, but by the time his long strides had carried him to the end of the street and the little town had dissolved into a few isolated cottages and fields, the words and phrases did come, and although he knew himself no scholar, he was more than half pleased with their verve and polish.

From time to time he was passed by carts and wagons, and once by the London coach proceeding on its way south at a stately pace that made him once again recall Joan's reasoning. When he came to the place in the road where the carrier had reported finding the priest's body, he poked around in the thorny brake with his staff, hoping to find evidence, but he found only the imprint of a body in the grass and a spot of blood, now dried and brown.

By the time the Hall came within his view, he was breathing heavily, for he had walked the distance in less than an hour by the sun. It was the groom who answered the door. He led Matthew through the gloomy high-ceilinged corridor to a small chamber he had not seen before and knocked twice. When a voice inside responded, the groom vanished into the darkness and the clothier entered to find himself in a small office where he was greeted coldly by Varnell.

"Saltmarsh and his lady have departed this hour for London," Varnell snapped, obviously enjoying his pre-eminence in the house now that his master and mistress were gone. "I join them myself tomorrow, when I have finished up some of my employer's business."

"Then I have come too late," Matthew said inaudibly, his heart heavy with disappointment.

"You what?" the secretary said.

"I am come to report another death, that of your master's guest."

The secretary looked up suddenly; a strange expression passed across his face and then vanished into a sneer. He said, "I thought Sir Henry dismissed you as constable."

"Indeed he has. Yet I remain a citizen of the town."

Varnell's eyes came alive with curiosity. "Who found the body, and in what condition?"

"His body was found early this morning, by the wayside not a mile below this house. He had been struck by a cart or coach, and drug a good distance, I should judge."

The secretary turned pale and spoke hesitantly. "I will bear the news to Sir Henry tomorrow. He will be grieved to hear that a friend has met death so unfortunately."

"It was not an accident," Matthew said bluntly.

"What, no accident? How so?"

"The circumstances do not fit the event. The night was clear of clouds and the moon full."

"And from such you conclude foul play," the secretary responded. His penchant for mockery had returned; he had stopped trembling.

Matthew continued: "Aye, and yet when joined with other things—"

"What other things?" the secretary interrupted.

"The other deaths."

"The one died of her own hands, of grief 'tis likely. The other remains unsolved. How connect you those two deaths with this?"

Matthew hesitated. The secretary had quickly come to the root of it, which he must now pull up, if only to save his own pride.

"Someone from the Hall came to fetch Richard Mull, the night he was murdered. I've proof of it, if proof be needed."

"And?"

"Saltmarsh reported no theft of horses."

The secretary turned his back on the constable, stood looking from his tiny window into the desolate garden. "Still you draw conclusions from no substantial evidence."

"I conclude," Matthew returned sharply, "that this house has within this week become a place of death sufficient to alarm the folk of this town and justify the concern of the law."

"Harry Saltmarsh *is* the law," Peter Varnell screeched, turning to face him.

"Harry Saltmarsh is not the law," Matthew returned with equal force. "He has been given charge of its rule hereabouts, no more, and is subject to it as much as the next man."

The secretary seated himself behind the desk and began to play with his long fingers. The light in the room was bad; Matthew could not discern the man's expression.

"I will inform Sir Henry of the death of his friend," Varnell said more calmly. "If you wish to convey aught else to him you may, but for my part I have nothing to report to him beyond your own remarks, which I believe he will hardly find pleasing in one who at this point has his nose well into business that is no longer his concern."

The secretary picked from a pile a sheaf of papers and began to write. At first Matthew thought it might be a note for him; then he realized that he was deliberately being ignored, that the interview was over. So, Matthew thought, it is finished. Perhaps the man was right, justice must bow to power; and in this case the power was certainly Saltmarsh's. Matthew sought a closing word, something to restore the dignity of his presence, but he could find nothing to the purpose. Humiliated, he turned and found his own way out.

Varnell read the same few lines over and over before giving it up as a bad job. Now he could think of nothing but the dead priest. He had not liked the man. He had perceived him to be but another threat to his own desired intimacy with the Saltmarshes, and particularly with his mistress. And yet he identified with him. They were near enough to the same age, they had sat at table together, and the man's ambitions were doubtless of a kind the secretary might appreciate, for he supposed it as fine a thing to be a bishop as be lord temporal. Despite what he had told the constable, Varnell could well believe the priest's death no accident. The idea of murder did not bother his conscience or disturb his sense of social propriety. He was now quite beyond such moral queasiness. What disturbed him was the discovery that here was a murder carried out close to home to which he was not a party and for a motive quite unknown to him. What might the priest have done to deserve this? Slandered Harry Saltmarsh, threatened his life, violated his bed?

At the moment fear clenched his heart. He imagined himself standing naked before his employer, all of his sexual fantasies open to an outraged husband's inspection. Saltmarsh had never really struck him as a jealous man, despite the reason he had given the secretary for wanting the players' boy dead. Yet perhaps the quieter sort were the most dangerous. He had never been married himself; how could he know what suspicions lurked in a married man's heart, especially an older man with a young wife? Quickly he reviewed the events of the past week, seeking some incidental action of his own that might have provided Saltmarsh with a revelation of his secretary's lust. There was nothing, nothing that he could recall, and yet perhaps there need be nothing. His employer was a strange man. Peter Varnell would have felt so much better could he only know for certain just what was going on.

He labored over his fears until the servingman came to inform him that dinner was served, and it was not until he had scratched at his plate—he ate alone—that it occurred to him that he might be possessed by idle fears no more substantial than his imaginary affair with Cecilia Saltmarsh. He had, after all, no proof that Saltmarsh was behind the priest's death, only the suspicions of the constable and his own guilty conscience as a presumptive adulterer. His new awareness brought relief; he quickly finished his food before him and called to the kitchen for a second serving and another bottle of wine.

After dinner he returned to his chamber and finished copying a long letter—the last of his duties. This and other documents he placed neatly in his chest, where they would not be damaged during the journey to London. Then he made a final inspection of the small room to see if he had left anything behind him which he might require. As he did so, and in a much lighter mood, he once again contemplated his own future. His fears, he concluded now that his stomach was full and his head light with wine, had not been ridiculous; they were in fact quite understandable. Saltmarsh was a dangerous man, willful, arrogant, and murderous if such would advance his cause, but so were all great men to Peter Varnell's mind. He must bear such risks. Besides, he should have hated it had his idle fancies deprived him of the comfortable social position he now enjoyed, one that might prove even more comfortable once he was situated in London, where his diligence might come to the attention of even greater persons. At the thought his heart swelled almost to overflowing and he wished for the moment that he might believe in some god again so as to have a divinity to thank for his good fortune.

The next morning the sun flooded his chamber. He gathered his things and called for the groom, who somewhat resentfully helped him carry his chest to the front of the house and to the cart waiting beyond. He made a note to himself to speak to his employer about the man, and later at parting handed him but a single shilling for his pains, rather than the two he had intended in an earlier and more generous mood.

Just as Peter Varnell hailed the London coach, his master and mistress were near halfway to their destination, riding comfortably in their own coach, with the Saltmarsh crest emblazoned on the door and at its top piled high with Cecilia Saltmarsh's luggage.

They had been silent through the earlier part of their journey. She had stared sullenly at the passing scene; he had been engrossed in a book, a small volume of verse. The day was pleasant, the weather having turned for the better. Harry Saltmarsh would have been quite content had it not been for the painful itching in his groin. The rash had bothered him for weeks, but only in the last few days had it become a great vexation. Well, it was the French pox, he concluded, which a trip to Madame Mercury's baths could cure after he arrived in London.

Cecilia Saltmarsh also anticipated her arrival in London, but for entirely different reasons. She was growing weary of her husband and was at that instant contemplating their future together. She was done with his tricks; she would have no more blood on her hands. She would still have admirers, lovers, and she might even be satisfied by them, but she would accomplish this without her husband's supervision. Perhaps, she supposed, he would find the city large and diverse enough to satisfy his appetite for curious pleasures. Let him do so, so he might leave her be.

He was the first to break their long silence, with a comment that immediately set her teeth on edge.

"You are thinking of how you may spend my money in the city?" His tone was polite, but she knew the intent of the question and felt her face flush with anger.

She said, "I think my own thoughts, and to this minute had pleasure in them."

"Well, then, if 'tis my silence you prefer, you shall have it aplenty in London, for my business will keep me away most nights."

"I trust they will." She sneered.

They nursed their mutual enmity in silence; then her husband spoke again. "I have but one satisfaction as I reflect on the events of this week. That is that in all things you were my partner."

She turned to him coldly, searching the heavy features of the nose and chin, the leathery flesh. "You are generous with your guilt," she said. "Be not too content, though. I love you only for your wealth and place. Were it not for those, I should gladly keep company with your enemies."

"At least you realize what I provide for you," he replied, his heavy lips curling into a smirk. He turned to stare at the passing countryside, as though she had done no more than remark upon the weather.

"You have bound me to you," she continued with bitterness in her voice. "I daily enumerate the ways, as others count their beads. Yes, I like the conceit. 'Tis all like my rosary. My devotion is a prayer to some obscure saint that you may one day be hanged."

He brought the back of his hand sharply across her cheek. She drew back in her seat, startled, her face burning. She could taste blood in her mouth, but she contained her tears of rage. She would give him no satisfaction, let him do what he will. She turned from him. There were more cottages now, more traffic upon the road. In the distance she could see smoke of the great city. Slowly she reconstructed her dignity.

"You are a man; I am only a woman and may not stay your anger. But you depend on me as I on you, and God knows why. We will not remain forever in London. We will return to Chelmsford, and when we do you will have need of me again. If I am to be your fellow in your tricks, then you had best treat me civilly, or I may forget what debt I owe you."

"And do what?" he asked threateningly.

She did not respond to his question; she wanted to give him time to consider the possibilities himself. His face was frozen in a smile of the sort bodies sometimes bear in the rigor of death.

She said, "I will not tell you now. Much depends on how I am treated henceforth."

The coach came to a halt; the driver called down that they had arrived at the inn where they would dine.

"I am hungry," her husband said without emotion, as though nothing had passed between them.

The driver, a busy little man with whiskers the color of straw, dismounted and held the door open for his mistress, who cast her husband one last threatening glance before extending her hand to meet her servant's. The driver, seeing the purplish bruise on her right cheek and the swollen lip, averted his gaze. Then Harry Saltmarsh dismounted. He gave the driver a look of warning and sent the man scurrying toward the stable to find a hostler.

The walk home was longer. Matthew had missed his dinner, but not for that reason alone was his heart heavy. He found the shop full of customers efficiently served by Joan and one of the apprentices. He nodded to those he knew, then buried himself in his accounts until the light was spent, the shop closed, and supper called.

Joan had not bothered him with questions; he had marveled at that, for he well knew her curiosity. They spoke instead of family things—of the crock Alice broke, of daughter's new husband, of the last vestiges of summer's garden, now dry and sere. When the supper was done and the table cleared, they passed from the kitchen up the stairs to their own bedchamber.

"Have you had enough of my brooding?" he asked, looking into her gray eyes.

"If you must brood more, then be it so," she said, making the bed ready. "I will not force you to speak of what you would not."

He smiled, quite without wanting to. A black mood was still upon him, but he knew her means of having her way while seeming to allow him his.

He said, "The Saltmarshes have left for London. There's no more to be done."

"You found the Hall empty, then?"

"Only the groom with the long face and Master Varnell. With him I spoke briefly but to no good end."

Then he rehearsed his conversation with the secretary, surprised at how quickly, once he had come to the telling of it, his story was done.

Joan listened attentively, nodding now and again to confirm his impressions or to express dismay or sympathy. She said, "You are right. There's no help for it now. But I think Master Varnell knows well of his master's wickedness. What choice had he but to defend him? To make you think your suspicions were no more than an illusion?"

"Yet he was right in this," Matthew said, "that we had no proof, nothing that a court would give an ear to much less bring a conviction upon. I doubt not but that it would go hard with me were I to press a charge against a clear gentleman of name and land—and the magistrate to boot."

He dropped his hands into his lap in a gesture of defeat. The firelight played upon their faces so that the lines of age were exaggerated and the features sharpened. A mouse, perhaps drawn by the fire's warmth, scurried beneath their chairs, taking refuge near the wood box, and watched them fearfully with its small black eyes. Silent, but not uncommunicative, Joan reached over to place her hands in Matthew's. At last she spoke, shaping into words the answer to her own unspoken question.

"You will sell cloth and keep honest accounts and I bake

161

bread and pray for grandchildren. 'Tis no more nor less than we have done before . . . before the boy's death and we knew nothing more of the Hall than the way there. God has made a world in which Harry Saltmarsh may have his wickedness; let God then judge the man and see to his punishment.''

"Do you remember old Jupiter in the play? Such a god would not have suffered such evil.''

"Though he might have practiced it himself,'' she responded wittily, although she could read in his face that her cleverness had gone unnoticed. "It is impious to compare the two,'' she said more seriously, trying to find her way back to his own mood. "Besides, 'twas only a play. There justice must be done that the folk may homeward full of sound doctrine. The world is not a stage.''

" 'Tis late,'' he said, feeling more weary than he had ever in his life before. "Come, Joan, you and I are older than we were, and maybe no wiser. Let's go pray and then to bed. Tomorrow I will reckon my accounts and you bake your bread, and if daughter be not with child by that son-in-law of mine we shall make him answer to it.''

She laughed with him, realizing that if his gloom had not been driven from the house it had at least been tempered by his normal cheerfulness. He was struggling—for her sake as well as his own—and she loved him for that and for the vexation of spirit and outrage that pained him now and would pain them many times before their posterity would weep over their graves.

13

THE WINTER came and went, and life for the Stocks pursued its normal course. No longer constable, Matthew looked to his business and Joan to the house. Daughter Elizabeth and her husband moved into a pretty cottage at the end of High Street, giving the Stocks much company on cold December nights. But about the Saltmarsh affair, Matthew held his peace. Joan understood his silence, respected it, but she watched knowingly. Meanwhile the Saltmarshes did not return to the Hall. Then in early April Matthew had a letter from Big Tod and Gwen, who were now settled in London. They were well, the letter said. The theaters were full, and they had seen the Saltmarshes, man and wife, riding proudly one afternoon through the London streets.

For a few days after, Matthew brooded. He ignored his accounts and custom, paced the floors, stared stonily from the window into the street. Finally he could contain himself no longer. He would be off to London that very day. He declared that he should not sleep soundly ever again in his life if Henry Saltmarsh were to go free. To this, Joan put up no argument. She called Alice to prepare the master's bag and fetch some cheese and ale for the journey. She saw to his cloak herself, saying, "Look to yourself. Sir Henry is bound to have powerful friends who will not take your pursuit of him kindly."

He nodded his agreement, securing his cloak to his shoulders and then making sure his purse was full and fast to his belt. "I'll lodge at the Blue Boar without Aldgate. The wagons from Chelmsford do come there on Wednesdays. If I have not returned by then send Samuel—"

She interrupted, "I'll send myself, not Samuel. Keep you warm."

Alice brought the bag while Matthew and Joan embraced. Then he hurried into the street and down to the corner where the London coach passed every afternoon at one o'clock. He paid his fare to the driver, boarded the coach, and sat by a window. He watched the street rush by, a sprinkling of familiar faces, the clearing sky in the west and greening hills of emergent spring. This was the world of his childhood, of his life. His heart sank as he thought of Joan and Elizabeth. He wondered momentarily if he were experiencing a presentiment of his own death, and shuddered. But now in open country the black mood passed. Headed southward, he laid his plans, and soon, lulled by the monotonous beat of hooves upon the road, he fell into an unquiet sleep.

The Blue Boar was cheap but convenient. Matthew secured a dark room under the eaves. He needed nothing fancy; his stay would be brief. His plan was to appeal to some great lord, to somehow surmount Saltmarsh's little tyranny. If that failed, then he would admit defeat and homeward straightway. He would bury his knowledge in his heart. God would dispose.

On the day following his arrival he went directly to an old acquaintance who had left Chelmsford for London years earlier to seek his fortune. The friend had begun as apprentice to a butcher, become in due time his master's heir, and ended as an investor in foreign trade. He had been as far as Muscovy and had returned the richer. Most important, he knew his way about the city and was acquainted with influential persons at court.

Matthew's friend lived in a spacious new house in an

elegant quarter of the city. Luckily he was at home when Matthew called, happy to oblige, if only to display his influence, and having heard an abbreviated account of Matthew's purpose, to furnish him with a letter of introduction to Master Giles, the secretary of Sir Robert Cecil, who was Secretary of State. But the friend gave Matthew little hope. Amused at the clothier's earnestness, he observed cynically that if murder were all Saltmarsh were guilty of he might expect rather to die an earl than a mere knight, for surely it was a wicked world. Indeed, he knew worse of two privy councillors and a bishop. Crestfallen, Matthew thanked the man for the letter and left.

He spent most of the afternoon discovering that Robert Cecil was not in London; then he rented a horse and rode two hours for Theobalds, where he had been informed the great lord had retired to read and hunt. There, dismounting before a broad avenue of elm and ash still barren of leaves, Matthew stared at the great house with its high square towers and many mullioned windows ablaze in the late afternoon sun, thinking all the while that the house was more fit for a king than for a courtier. The liveried servant who took his horse looked at his letter to Master Giles contemptuously and led him to a side entrance, muttering something about the lateness of the hour and looking askance at Matthew's shabby suit and dusty boots.

He was led down several long passages into a small windowless chamber occupied by a young well-dressed man seated primly at a desk with pen in hand and face resting in his palm. The only other occupant in the chamber, after the servant had turned away, was a gray-bearded man of Matthew's years and stature, looking very downcast and holding a file of papers tightly to his chest as though he expected any moment to have it snatched from him. The young man—Master Giles, Matthew supposed—motioned him to a bench. After a few minutes of silence, the gentleman with the file rose wearily, approached the clerk, whispered something in his ear to which the young man shook his head firmly, and then walked past Matthew and through the door the clothier had just entered. Matthew waited while the young man wrote in a book, sharpened his quill, stared vacantly into space. But he did not once look up at Matthew.

It was nearly an hour before the secretary spoke, beckoning him forward and then studying his letter of introduction as though it had been composed in a foreign tongue.

"Your business with Master Giles?"

"You are not he?" Matthew began, quite bewildered.

The secretary looked up with hard eyes. "I am his lordship's secretary's secretary," he responded matter-of-factly, his gaze falling again to Matthew's letter. "Your business?"

"My business is with Master Giles," Matthew said dryly.

The secretary snorted and continued to peruse the letter while Matthew waited with growing impatience. The air in the room was stale; tobacco smoke, he thought, a vile thing he thanked God had yet to find its way to Chelmsford.

The secretary at last looked up. "Master Giles has left for the day."

"When will he return?"

"Tomorrow, perhaps. You may return yourself then if you really feel your business with him merits it."

Matthew tried to ignore the insolence of the reply, folding and unfolding his moist hands behind him. But then he could contain himself no longer; he had ridden too far and waited too long. "You are Master Giles's secretary and you know so little of his affairs that you cannot tell me plainly whether he will return tomorrow or no?"

The young man drained of color, his hard eyes narrowed. "I said what I have said," he replied flatly, placing Matthew's letter of introduction within the drawer of his desk and locking it with a tiny key he had drawn in an instant from his laced cuff.

"May I have my letter back?" Matthew asked.

"The letter is addressed to Master Giles. I will show it to him when 'tis convenient."

Matthew had begun to protest, when suddenly he became aware of movement behind him. The servant who had brought him hither had returned along with two burly companions. The three stood with their arms folded, their eyes hostile. Intimidated, Matthew turned to the secretary. "I am indebted to you, sir, for your courtesy." He did not bother to conceal his vexation.

The secretary nodded to the servants, and Matthew stepped out carefully between the brawny shoulders of the servingman and his companions and proceeded down what he thought was the same narrow passage he had entered. Behind him he could hear the muffled laughter of the men, and his face reddened with anger. As he opened the door at the end of the passage, he emerged not into the courtyard as he had expected but found himself at the end of still another passage. Confused, he pushed on, not wishing to humiliate himself further by returning to inquire directions of the undersecretary. After a few steps he came to yet another door. Upon opening it, he found himself in a large well-appointed chamber hung with tapestries and portraits, an office of sorts, but certainly not that of an undersecretary. Before Theobalds, he would have thought it fit for the Queen; now in light of what he had already seen, he supposed it might well be the chamber of the elusive Master Giles. The room itself had many doors, some of which he presumed were closets. He realized that he was passing deeper into the great house and that now he had no alternative but to push on. Perhaps he could find another servant who would doubtless be all too ready to show him the way out.

He walked about the chamber listening for voices in unseen chambers beyond but heard nothing. Finally he selected a door at random and opened it.

Before him was the richness of summer—trees in their pride, fully leaved and heavy with fruit. He stared incredulously. Then high above he saw the ornate vaulted ceiling and realized he was in an immense room. The trees lining the walls had been fashioned by some marvelously clever artisan. Over his head an artificial sun traced the path of the zodiac.

He was about to reach out for a golden pear partially hidden in a clump of brightly enameled leaves, when he heard a voice behind him. "Nay, 'tis forbidden fruit."

Matthew turned abruptly. The command had come from

a recess in the wall. As he was considering the possibility that the voice too was an illusion, its owner—a splendidly dressed young man with broad forehead and shapely pointed beard—materialized from behind a potted shrub. The young man eyed Matthew curiously. A handsome man, Matthew thought, his slightly hunched back was more the pity.

"Master Giles?" Matthew asked, having found his own voice at last.

"Master Cecil," the lord of Theobalds replied, smiling wryly.

Sir Robert Cecil composed himself at his desk, his delicate hands assuming the shape of a cathedral spire and pressing against his thin lips. "Your evidence, Master Stock, lacks credit, without which any accusation against Sir Henry Saltmarsh and his lady is more likely to accrue danger to you than to them."

"I know, Sir Robert, that I be no more than a former town constable and that those who would swear against Sir Henry are humble folk like unto myself. But that they would swear truly I would pledge my life."

"Your earnestness I doubt not," Cecil said after a moment's pause. "But I can do nothing for you. This business is not a matter of state. It is a local affair."

Matthew, who rose with his august host, felt his heart sink within him. When Sir Robert had consented to speak with him despite the lateness of the hour and the inconvenience of the interruption of what he had called his hour of meditation, he was sure he had come to both the end and the reward of his effort. Now it would seem he was at an end without reward. Justice was hardly closer than it had been before he left Chelmsford in this last, desperate attempt.

"Then the murderer of the players' boy and the priest must go free," Matthew said beneath his breath.

"What is that you say?" Cecil asked with sudden interest.

Matthew repeated himself.

"You said nothing before of a priest."

Matthew proceeded to explain how the priest's body had been found in the road and his relationship with the Saltmarshes as reported by Gwen Mair.

"Quickly, then, describe this priest. How tall a man was he? Of what years and complexion?"

Matthew did so to the best of his memory, puzzled by the excitement his mention of the priest had occasioned. Then Cecil rang a little golden bell on his desk. Within seconds, a tall angular man with bushy eyebrows and blank expression stepped quietly and efficiently into the chamber and was listening attentively to something his master was whispering into his right ear. The man with the bushy eyebrows passed out of the chamber as quietly as he had entered, only to return instantly with a file of documents which he proceeded to lay out before his master. From the file, Cecil pulled what appeared to be a letter, held it to the light, and muttered the name "Hayforth" beneath his breath.

"It would appear I do know your knight somewhat better than I recalled," Cecil said after a few moments of reflection.

"Sir?"

"Your Sir Henry's Papist sympathies have been noted. Though no great devil, he is nonetheless one whose activities have borne watching. This letter confirms the serving girl's account of his hospitality to the priest, who was, by the way, a priest in appearance only. Indeed, he has been for more than a dozen years one of our agents. This letter in his own hand confirms his English itinerary, including a projected visit to Saltmarsh Hall, Essex. This is his last report. He is dead, then?"

"I myself saw to his burial."

"The priest's involvement puts a new face on the matter," Cecil said coolly, reaching for a quill and beginning to scribble something.

Matthew watched the man's face intently. He was beginning to feel hopeful again, but he had been misled by hope so often he tried now to restrain his expectations. To Matthew, a murder was a murder. His sense of justice was not complicated by the drawing of distinctions between victims. But if this great man so knowledgeable in the law drew such, then he would not say nay, though the distinction be beyond his understanding.

"You will charge Sir Henry, then, with the murder of the priest?" Matthew asked finally.

"No, not murder, but for harboring a priest. 'Twill be an easier charge to confirm, and in some ways 'tis the more grievous. The state has lost little in the death of a players' boy. His place can be readily taken by five hundred tomorrow with prettier faces and sweeter voices. Nor is the priest's death much of a loss. An old spy grows stale. It has been five years since he was worth his keep. But to harbor a priest is to undermine the state—what stands between our liberty and the Pope's tyranny."

Cecil handed Matthew what he had been writing. It was a letter authorizing him to accompany a Queen's officer in the arrest of Sir Henry and Cecilia Saltmarsh and their secretary. "Go you now," he said. "My officer will have his warrant before noon tomorrow, and if the Saltmarshes be yet in London they shall have supper in the Tower."

Back at the inn, Matthew pulled off his boots and fell back on the bed, too weary to remove his coat. A fire had been laid in the grate, thank God for that. It had been a long day, the strangest of his life. Now he needed time to think, and he needed sleep despite the turmoil in his brain. After an hour's staring at the rafters, during which his mind wandered the dimly lit tortuous passages of the Saltmarsh business, he rose, went to his chamber's small table, took writing materials from his bag, and began a letter to Joan, careful to make his characters large and clear.

Writing helped him put his thoughts in order. It was comforting to think of Joan, of daughter Elizabeth, of their cheery house on High Street, of his busy and prosperous shop. In the letter he said nothing of Theobalds or Sir Robert Cecil. The explanation would have taken too long. Besides, he had no gift of expression. For now he wanted no more than to assure Joan of his safety and to inform her that things were going well. It gave him pleasure to save much for later when he could read her gray eyes and touch her with his hands. The writing made him sleepy at last.

He prayed that the Saltmarshes had not left the city. If they had, their apprehension might prove difficult. Besides, he wanted for all the world to be present at their arrest, not so much to see their fear as to see himself justified. While his imagination thus prophesied of things to come, he watched the fire burn low and finally die. He signed the letter, sealed it, and lay back on the bed. As the chamber grew colder, he yielded to sleep. Slowly the room became crowded with vague images of the day, partially concealed faces and muffled voices. He stood again before Theobalds and walked the maze of its corridors. In his gathering dream he reached out for a golden pear, luminescent on a shimmering green bough, brought it to his lips, and found the fruit delicious to his taste.

Matthew rode the water uneasily, perched in the bow of the boat. Before him sat Cecil's man, a captain of the Queen's guard, dressed in scarlet and girdled with a businesslike sword. With them were two pikemen, sturdy young fellows in the Queen's livery and bearing expressions of stolid determination. The captain grumbled to himself. The day was fair, full of the promise of the spring, but the air on the river was cold. Downstream, Matthew could see the great bridge of London; behind him the city itself unfolded like a mural. Ahead, on the approaching south bank of the river, Matthew saw the theater itself, rising above the thatched roofs of smaller houses like a stout keg of beer. A flag flew from its mast. Across the water came the sound of cannon fire.

"The play's begun," the captain said. "We'll take them indoors, worse luck. If we can make it through the gang of lords, gentlefolk, thieves, punks, and pickpurses that keep house at the Globe on such a day as this."

The tide was low, and the men steadied themselves as the bow of the boat nudged other boats pulled up in the mud. When the captain paid the waterman, the man cringed, taking his pay with ill-concealed dissatisfaction and casting a resentful look at Matthew, who at the moment was concentrating on his footing in the marshy bank. The trip across the river had been Matthew's first experience on water and he felt somewhat unsettled still, although he was not sure whether it was the river crossing or the expectation of the arrest that made his stomach churn.

They trudged up the bank to a flight of stairs and then down a lane intersected by foul-smelling ditches. Matthew had a full view of the theater now, a roundish building of timber and plaster rising a good thirty to forty feet in the midst of a scattering of trees and solid looking houses. Outside the theater, vendors of meat and drink had set up booths, giving the immediate area the look of a country fair. At the moment, however, the booths were empty: late patrons had crowded in front of the doors, pushing and shoving, holding out their pennies to the gatherer.

Matthew followed the captain as he pushed the latecomers aside while the gatherer with his money box took one look at the pikeman and without a word waved them through into the theater. Inside, it was as tumultuous as a bear-baiting. The yard was jammed to the walls with shirt-sleeved apprentices, countrymen, and poor gentlemen, elbowing each other for standing room and picking quarrels at random. Just above their heads, Matthew could see the stage, jutting out into the center of the great wooden "O" of the theater like a peninsula. Players—fools and jesters by their motley dress and rough and tumble motions—were entertaining the crowd with a comic swordfight. Around and above him, the galleries for the two-penny patrons rose in tiers to the open sky. Matthew screwed up his eyes in search of the Saltmarshes, but it was hopeless. He could see nothing but the backs of heads and the elegant hats of gallants. A coarse-faced cake vendor pushed her basket into his ribs. The place smelled foully of unwashed bodies and garlic to ward off the plague. Here and there tobacco smoke ascended to the sky.

One of the actors, a neatly dressed man with a frank, open face and clever eyes had been standing next to the money gatherer as they had entered. He introduced himself as the chief of the company and told them that although he did not know the knight and lady they sought, given their quality they would probably be seated in the lords' room, just above the stage for the superior view and fresher air. The captain thanked the actor and pushed Matthew ahead of him into the crowd. "Get you in front, Master Stock," the captain said, "and search the faces. I would not know this knight were he the second man in Eden and Adam dressed in a fig leaf."

Obediently, Matthew assumed the lead, the neatly-dressed actor having disappeared into the crowd, and began to make his way slowly forward, but he soon found advancing impossible. Impatient, the captain sent the pikeman forward to clear the way; and the standing patrons, seeing the armed soldiers, made a clearing, buzzing with resentment and staring at Matthew curiously. As they drew to the center of the crowd Matthew looked up at the great pillars behind the stage and recognized the face of Sir Henry's secretary staring down from the lords' room. He grasped the captain by the shoulder and pointed to where he had seen Varnell's face and then followed as the captain and his men pushed toward the stairs and began to climb to the upper gallery.

The gallery was full of bodies and noises. Fashionably dressed men and fewer women of quality were packed tightly together on the wooden benches gazing down to the stage, either lost in thought or convulsed in laughter. They fidgeted on their benches, called out to their friends, waved brightly colored handkerchiefs. A platoon of saucy, flamboyantly dressed women paraded the narrow passage between the benches and the theater walls beckoning to the gentlefolk or mocking each other. An old woman, her face a mask of white powder and her lips a grotesque red, blocked Matthew's path momentarily; her breath reeked of garlic. She said something inaudible and winked; her mouth twisted into a sneer. Matthew stepped around her and hurried to catch up with the captain and his guard, who had paused to wait for him before entering the lords' room. He followed them in, wondering how many crowded into that honored place were barons and earls. Then he saw Varnell again, and in the same second where Harry Saltmarsh and his wife were seated on comfortably cushioned benches and intent on the scene below.

Varnell was the first to look up, just as Matthew pointed him out and the captain and his men rushed forward with the arrest order. The secretary went pale. Cecilia Salt-marsh, who had turned toward the raised voices, stared at the captain, then at her husband, and finally at Matthew, her eyes widening with fright. Harry Saltmarsh was the last to realize what was going on; he turned languidly and looked at the captain, then immediately jumped to his feet at the same instant one of the pikemen moved forward to bind him. The two men struggled in the confined space, pushing Varnell hard against the wall and Cecilia Saltmarsh to the floor. Then somehow, despite the superior strength and number of officers, Harry Saltmarsh broke free, turned, mounted the railing, and leaped into the air.

Matthew and the captain rushed to the railing. Below, Saltmarsh had landed on the stage, his face contorted in pain; he looked about him confusedly, struggled to his feet while the audience, thinking the leap some curious sort of stage business, laughed and applauded wildly. The actors gawked at Saltmarsh and one another. None seemed to know just what to do. The gallants in the lower gallery hooted and threw their hats into the air.

Then Saltmarsh twisted his head back to look up at the lords' room. His wife had regained her footing and was bent over the railing staring down on the stage. She had covered her mouth with her hands. Below, her husband seemed immobilized by pain and confusion; only his thick lips moved, as though he were trying to frame an appeal or explanation. He turned to look at the audience around him. The crowd had fallen silent. Suddenly as though awakening from a dream, Saltmarsh rushed to the apron of the stage and thrust himself into a rout of apprentices who greeted his fall with howls of anger and derision.

As it turned out, Joan had not stayed for his letter. She had ordered Philip to hitch up the cart and the two of them had driven to London. She was waiting for Matthew when he returned to the inn late in the afternoon.

"I have news that could not wait," she said breathlessly, collapsing with weariness onto the bed.

"Indeed," Matthew replied after a proper greeting and an expression of wonder that she should have come so far.

"I think 'twas more likely your curiosity about matters here."

"Something has happened, then?" she said, her eyes widening.

"It has, but shall we have your news first?"

"No," she replied firmly. "We'll have yours first. I'll not have mine run a poor second. 'Tis too important."

"Well, then, Sir Henry, his lady, and the secretary were taken not two hours since. Sir Henry near broke his neck falling to the stage at the Globe. When I saw the secretary last, he was all aglisten with his sweat, shivering as though stark naked in a north wind, and confessing more than he was asked for by anyone accompanying him. The lady said nothing but looked as white as a corpse. The Queen's officers bore them all straightway to the Tower. I had my stomach full for the day of them all, so returned here, and a good thing too, since now you've come."

There was much more to tell her, of course, about the great house at Theobalds, his conversation with Cecil, and the excitement at the Globe, but it would keep for the ride home. She did not wait for him to invite her to speak her own news.

"Elizabeth is with child!"

"What say you?"

"Goose, Elizabeth, your daughter, is with child at last. Your son-in-law has done his duty by her and by us. What think you of that?"

He leaped from the bed and embraced her. "We shall be grandparents yet. You should not have delayed this. 'Twould have put me in a better mind."

She smiled with satisfaction, her arms around his waist. She said, "I supposed your having been to London would have put thoughts of home far from your head. What will you do now about the shop with no public charge save to keep the peace yourself?"

"Why, we shall grow old together. I'll teach my grandson to cipher and in due time to keep accounts. Come, help me with my bag. We'll leave forthwith and doze if we must in the cart."

"I will not," she said, her lips forming into a charming

pout. "This is my first trip to London and I will see the sights though I die of 'em. 'Twill be winter before I put on a grandmother's name. For now, I expect to see the old Queen, perhaps an earl or two, and a play if you please. Indeed," she said, warming to her theme, "I would see at least one play. Something cheery and with no offense in it. The innkeeper with whom I spoke below tells me of a new comedy at the Globe, by a Master Shakespeare, full of summer . . ."

14

Two days later it was snowing. It had taken them all by surprise, the wind having suddenly shifted, and now the snow had covered the streets. Already the smoke of city fires had turned the evening sky the color of undyed wool. Inside the tavern it was warm and crowded, for the weather had sent passersby scurrying for shelter; and having found jolly company indoors and drink and food, they stayed. By the large front window looking out on the street the players were huddled companionably about a long table. There was a great deal of shouting and some singing, a rowdy group of sailors quarreling at the bar, staid merchants exchanging news, toasting one another, haggling over the price of their wares, a puny effeminate Frenchman playing the virginals in the corner, his music lost in the general tumult. From everywhere there was the raucous call of the waiters and drawers, callow youth with servile expressions and insolent tongues.

At the moment Will Shipman was engaged in an animated discussion with Big Tod; they were, in fact, veering hard toward a quarrel. Gwen, her belly already betraying the rotundity of motherhood, was trying to calm her husband, but she had come late to the old antagonism between the two players. Neither would be pacified. Now the two were jaw to jaw while their fellows chose sides and quarreled among themselves. Then with a fist brought sharply down upon the table so that the blow spilled more than one cup, Will Shipman asserted his authority and the players fell into a respectful silence.

"Now," he said, "we shall not play where we will but where we can. We are best off hiring a private house or innyard, say for a share of the poke. When summer comes we'll be off to the country again. As for the plays we shall perform"—here Will paused for a drink and gauged the effect of his words—"we may do *Hieronimo*, which, though old, draws always a good crowd, or perhaps *Friar Bacon*. Myself, I prefer the tried and true rather than go with what may please some starving scholar's fancy."

"Then we will not do *Aeneas* again," Samuel Peacham lamented. "And here I have brought my part therein to perfection."

The little actor's remark, posed puckishly, brought the relief of laughter, which Gwen joined, having been for the most part of the afternoon overawed and certainly outvoiced by the masculine company.

"Nay," Will replied thoughtfully once the laughter and jibes had subsided. "I've no heart for it now."

Remembering Richard Mull, the others nodded in agreement. It had been five months, yet the death was green in their hearts.

Then Gwen cried, "Look, 'tis the constable and his lady, here in London."

They all looked toward the door. Matthew and Joan Stock, having in passing seen the players through the window, were making their way through the crowd. Will Shipman bellowed a greeting and beckoned them toward the table; the Stocks shed their caps and cloaks and in a moment all were seated in a joyful reunion, Joan having much to say to Gwen, noticing, as she immediately did, the young girl's condition.

"Why 'tis so with my Elizabeth!" she exclaimed. "I am heartily glad for you both."

Matthew was explaining to Will Shipman and the others

their reason for being in London. The Brothers Tod and Samuel Peacham were listening attentively, as were Joan and Gwen when the women realized where the conversation had drifted.

"So Harry Saltmarsh shall pay for his crime," Big Tod said triumphantly.

"Of that I have been assured," Matthew replied, having come within the hour from his second meeting with Cecil, this time in the great man's London chambers. "If not for the murders of the boy and the priest, then for his other crimes. Varnell has told everything and more in exchange for his skin."

Matthew recalled the meeting vividly. In a chamber of such intimidating grandeur that Saltmarsh's seemed a scrivener's closet by comparison, he had watched Cecil interrogate Varnell for nearly two hours. Pale, trembling, and disheveled, the secretary had not once glanced at Matthew. Instead his eyes were fixed on Cecil with a terrible fascination, as though he were about to fall upon his knees, not out of fear or reverence, but from sheer awe at such a concentration of power in a single mortal. The secretary had indeed told all, and in loathsome detail. Matthew had looked away for shame. The reciting of the acts curdled his blood. Cecil heard all with lordly detachment, his handsome features unmoved by passion. Varnell might have been a clerk summing up the great lord's accounts, or a groom recounting his treatment of an ailing mare. From time to time Cecil jotted down a word or phrase in a black leather book, less Matthew supposed to jog his memory than to terrify Varnell, whose eyes were red from weeping and whose voice periodically fell to a dry whisper. Then Varnell had been taken away, his fate uncertain.

"And what of my lady?" Gwen asked.

"Her husband's fall will be hers, too. Have no fear of that. When Sir Henry's acts become known, she'll not be eager to show her face out of doors."

" 'Tis all passing strange," Will Shipman mused. "I have never understood the half of it."

"Simon the hostler killed the boy," Matthew explained. "Richard Mull followed Varnell into the wood thinking he was being taken to the Hall for another meeting with his mistress. She and the boy were lovers. The hostler grabbed Richard by the neck and stabbed him while Varnell looked on. Then the two drug the body back to the stable so it would be thought one of you had killed him in a quarrel.''

"A devilish scheme," Big Tod exclaimed. "I wonder that Simon was willing to show you where the boy had met Varnell.''

"Blaming the murder on one of you was Varnell's idea. When I began to look into things at the inn, Simon grew frightened and was quick to point the finger elsewhere, even if there were the risk of having the murder laid upon him somewhere farther down the road.''

"Was it gold, then?" Will Shipman asked.

"In good part," Matthew replied. "Varnell procured the hostler on his employer's orders. 'Twas out of greed, but also ambition. The secretary had a great opinion of himself, was not content to remain the servant of a country knight, no matter how big a frog Saltmarsh was in our little pond. In that he was like many of our young scholars now, who for want of good breeding or secure employment think to climb to heaven by doing some great man's dirty work. They read all the Italian authors, I am told, and therein learn such villainy that 'twould make a pirate blush. As for the hostler, he hardly needed the lure of gold. He hated Richard Mull. I could tell it the first time I spoke to him at the inn. The boy was all that he was not—fair, straight of limb, and young. And beloved of the girl. That was the worst of it for him, for Simon wanted the girl himself. So he killed Richard Mull and, by the way, the girl too, she dying of grief as she did.''

"Which brings us then to Sir Henry," Gwen added.

"Ah yes," Joan ventured, for of that particular question she had been thinking much during their two days in London. Her husband was content to allow her to proceed; she thrust her elbows forward on the table, confidently and began:

"Harry Saltmarsh was unhappy in his affections. He would have loved is wife if he could, but she gave him no pleasure and she knew it. 'Twas no fault of hers, rather something lacking in her husband. She hated him every day of their marriage and let him know it. And he abused her foully, encouraging her to take lovers because that gave him a strange sort of satisfaction. Yet it also vexed his spirit. He lusted after the boy, made him his tool in the curious war he waged with his wife, and finally, fearing the boy might bear tales or wearying of the game, he ordered Richard Mull killed. Nothing pleased him at last but having his way. There's a moral in that," she concluded soberly, "though I am not sure yet exactly what it may be."

"But it is hard to believe a woman would act so unnaturally," Samuel Peacham said, his pinched face looking fairy-like wedged between the larger forms of Big Tod and Will Shipman.

Big Tod let out a cynical guffaw, upon which his little wife reached across the table to slap his face playfully.

"Such wickedness," Will Shipman said seriously.

"Our piety," Joan ventured again, "must make us call Harry Saltmarsh a wicked man, but were we to probe his heart we might find more the unhappy man, with so great and piteous a flaw that all else proceeded from it. His great powers were no blessing to him, nor his money. Had he been poor, he might have wasted his soul in mere vanities. As 'twas, his high place made him a great devil. His fall will be the farther."

"So he is in the Tower, then?" Little Tod said in what was more a statement than a question.

"I am told that he is so," Matthew responded, thinking again of his meeting with Cecil.

"Shall they hang him or will he rot, as they say some great ones do waiting the dispositions of their cases for years?"

"Who can know?" Big Tod said, taking his wife by the hand and pulling her toward him. "I have little faith in the law or in them administering it, but look rather to my own right arm."

"Whatever heaven accord," Joan said, "we can trust that all will rightly end, as we will see if we have the patience."

"And what of you, Master Constable?" Will Shipman asked good-humoredly. "Will you now be content after all of this great business and mingling with lords to mind your shop, or must you now make your livelihood the catching of wrongdoers? I should think counting rolls of cloth would now be as dull to you as herding sheep or mowing hay."

Matthew Stock laughed pleasantly. "I do dream of my shop ever, as Joan here will affirm."

But Joan smiled subtly and said nothing, content on this occasion to let her husband speak for himself.

"I am hungry," Matthew announced after more small talk at the table. "Surely this tavern must have an upper room where a company such as we be might eat. I think I have sufficient in my pocket." Matthew made a great show of searching for his purse, found it, opened it, and to the delight of all announced that there was indeed enough, though he and Joan might have to walk the way back to Chelmsford.

"I'm for the best part of a pig," Big Tod declared. "And my wife, too, for now she must eat for twain."

Matthew called for the tavern keeper, a big, burly man in a wine-stained smock and with a companionable grin. There was room indeed, and ready too, one large enough for them all and with a cheery fire. And there was a pig that he assured Matthew would be ready not half hour after the company had gathered upstairs. In the meantime there would be drinks aplenty and good fellowship.

Outside the snow had stopped and in the streets there was a festive air, as before some great holiday. The snow would not stay on the ground; it was spring and a jocund summer would soon follow. Matthew and Joan watched it as in a vision through the window while the company found their places at the table and the drawers brought the first round of ale. Somewhere below them they could hear the martial rhythms of a flute and drum, then the plaintive strains of a song. The quarreling sailors had made peace at last; some of the merchants had joined in, forgetting their trade. It was an old song of the country Matthew knew well.

"Nay, I know not the words." Joan flustered when her husband encouraged her to sing.

"No matter, no matter," Matthew replied, and then he began to sing in that mellifluous tenor that gave his neighbors in Chelmsford so much pleasure.

About the Author

LEONARD TOURNEY teaches at the University of Oklahoma. He is author of three other Constable Matthew Stock mysteries: THE BARTHOLOMEW FAIR MURDERS, FAMILIAR SPIRITS, and LOW TREASON.

Attention Mystery and Suspense Fans

Do you want to complete your collection of mystery and suspense stories by some of your favorite authors? John D. MacDonald, Helen MacInnes, Dick Francis, Amanda Cross, Ruth Rendell, Alistar MacLean, Erle Stanley Gardner, Cornell Woolrich, among many others, are included in Ballantine/Fawcett's new Mystery Brochure.

For your FREE Mystery Brochure, fill in the coupon below and mail it to: